Meet the police officers of the True Blue K-9 Unit series and their brave K-9 partners

Officer: Faith Johnson

K-9 Partner: Ricci the German shepherd

Assignment: Figure out who killed her ex-husband before the killer comes after her daughter

Officer: Teddy Kowalski

K-9 Partner: Garfunkel the Belgian Malinois

Assignment: Keep K-9 unit tech expert Danielle Abbot safe and put the person after her behind bars

Laura Scott is a nurse by day and an author by night. She has always loved romance and read faith-based books by Grace Livingston Hill in her teenage years. She's thrilled to have published over twenty-five books for Love Inspired Suspense. She has two adult children and lives in Milwaukee, Wisconsin, with her husband of over thirty years. Please visit Laura at laurascottbooks.com, as she loves to hear from her readers.

Maggie K. Black is an award-winning journalist and romantic suspense author with an insatiable love of traveling the world. She has lived in the American South, Europe and the Middle East. She now makes her home in Canada with her history-teacher husband, their two beautiful girls and a small but mighty dog. Maggie enjoys connecting with her readers at maggiekblack.com.

TRUE BLUE
K-9 UNIT
CHRISTMAS

LAURA SCOTT
MAGGIE K. BLACK

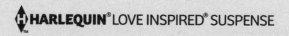

HARLEQUIN® LOVE INSPIRED® SUSPENSE

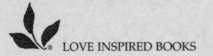 LOVE INSPIRED BOOKS

ISBN-13: 978-1-335-23249-6

True Blue K-9 Unit Christmas

Copyright © 2019 by Harlequin Books S.A.

Special thanks and acknowledgment are given to Laura Scott and Maggie K. Black for their contribution to the True Blue K-9 Unit series.

Holiday Emergency
Copyright © 2019 by Harlequin Books S.A.

Crime Scene Christmas
Copyright © 2019 by Harlequin Books S.A.

www.Harlequin.com

Printed in U.S.A.

CONTENTS

HOLIDAY EMERGENCY

Laura Scott

This book is dedicated to my new son-in-law,
Michael Collins, and his son, Lucas.
We are blessed to have you as part of our family.

For unto you is born this day in the city of David a Saviour, which is Christ the Lord. And this shall be a sign unto you; Ye shall find the babe wrapped in swaddling clothes, lying in a manger.
—*Luke* 2:11-12

ONE

Paramedic Pete Stallings peered through the fat snow-flakes in an attempt to find the spot along the Jackie Robinson Parkway where an injured man waited. The bright Christmas lights hanging from the streetlamps were almost obliterated by the falling snow.

There!

He yanked the wheel to pull over to the side of the road behind the squad car and threw the gearshift into Park.

"Let's go." Ignoring the wet snow melting on the nape of his neck he hurried to the back of the rig. It was disconcerting to have the crime scene so close to his home in the Forest Hills neighborhood of Queens, but he thrust the thought aside.

His partner, Kim Turner, was waiting when he opened the side-by-side doors. Together, they carried the gurney over the snowbank to where the uniformed officer was waving them down. As they grew closer, Pete could see the body of a man lying in bloodstained snow with a bleeding abdominal wound covered by a towel placed by the cop on the scene.

"I need dressings, lots of them," Pete told Kim. He was worried that an artery had been nicked and if they didn't stop the bleeding soon, their patient would die.

Kim opened their pack and handed over large squares of gauze. The man's eyes were open, and Pete could tell he was trying to talk.

"Take it easy." Pete tried to sound reassuring. "You'll be fine."

"Danger—keep her safe…" Their patient's voice was so faint, Pete could barely hear him.

"Who?" Pete couldn't tell if the guy was delirious or not. "Keep who safe?"

The man opened his mouth to answer, but then his mouth went slack and he closed his eyes without uttering another word.

A chill snaked down Pete's back and he resisted the urge to glance over his shoulder into the snowy field beyond. Was the assailant nearby? It was only three in the afternoon, but with the heavy clouds overhead it felt much later. The cops should have cleared the area, but he knew from experience anything was possible. He put pressure on the bleeding wound and leaned down to speak close to the man's ear. "Who? Keep who safe?"

Nothing. Their patient was unconscious. From the corner of his eye, he took note that Kim had started an IV. Fluids alone wouldn't be enough. He quickly checked for a pulse. It was faint and slow, a bad sign. Normally hypothermia helped stop bleeding but it could also be dangerous if the patient's temperature dropped too low.

"We're losing him," he warned.

"Logan! What happened? Who hurt him?" A female voice pleaded from behind him, but Pete didn't bother to look. He continued leaning on the wound while trying to help place the EKG leads on the guy's chest.

"We need to get him into the rig," Kim said as she squeezed the bag of fluids in an effort to raise the guy's blood pressure. "He's not going to make it if we don't get him to the hospital."

"I know." Pete lifted the pressure from the wound in order to help lift him onto the gurney, but instantly the EKG flatlined. He initiated CPR, knowing it was likely a fruitless effort. Their patient had already lost too much blood. Fluids weren't going to be enough and calling for a chopper wasn't an option.

Pete kept doing CPR, working up a sweat despite the chilly December afternoon. This guy was going to die less than a week before Christmas and there wasn't anything he could do to stop it.

"Hold CPR long enough to get him on the gurney," Kim directed.

He didn't want to stop, but knew they had to move. He paused long enough to lift their patient onto the gurney, then continued chest compressions. Kim secured the straps around the guy's body then gave him two breaths of oxygen through a face mask. Pete stopped CPR again so they could wheel him over the slick, snow-covered terrain to the rig.

"Wait! I'm a cop! I want to go with him." The female voice he'd heard earlier was louder now, but he continued to ignore her. The minute he had the patient stowed in the back of the rig, Pete jumped in beside him.

"I'll do CPR while you drive," he told Kim. CPR was hard work; he figured it made more sense for him to continue with performing chest compressions since he had fifty pounds on Kim and several inches.

The female cop with short, chin-length dark hair jumped into the back of the rig. A beautiful black-and-gold German shepherd joined her. "I know CPR. I can help," she said.

There wasn't time to argue, especially since he knew cops were trained in basic first aid. Pete resumed doing compressions while the female cop provided oxygen through a face mask.

"Come on, Logan. Hang on," she murmured.

Pete continued to count compressions out loud for her benefit. They reached the hospital quickly, and a team of doctors and nurses came out to meet them. They all rushed into the trauma bay, but less than five minutes later, it was over.

The doc on duty pronounced their patient dead.

Pete was sad and frustrated as he washed up, getting rid of the worst of the bloodstains before joining his partner. Since the pretty cop had called their patient by name, he figured they knew each other, but wasn't sure what their relationship was. When he approached Kim, the female cop was there with wide, sad eyes.

"I'm sorry for your loss." He knew the words were inadequate. After he'd lost his wife seven months ago, people had said the same thing and it hadn't made him feel any better.

"Thanks. Logan is my ex-husband." The cop's blue eyes shimmered with tears. "I'm not sure how I'm going to tell our daughter he's gone."

In that moment he placed her, belatedly recognizing her from the day-care center where his son, Mikey, went to a pre-K program. "Faith Johnson," he said. "From the day-care center. You're Jane's mom."

She sniffled and wiped at her eyes, managing a weak smile. "Yes. And I should have recognized you as Mikey's dad. Jane talks about Mikey all the time."

"Same here." Suddenly, the last words Logan had spoken took on a new meaning.

Keep her safe.

Pete wondered if Logan had been talking about his

ex-wife. Had Logan been involved in something illegal? Drugs? Guns? Something that now put his ex-wife at risk?

"Faith, can I speak to you privately for a moment?" Pete glanced pointedly at Kim who sighed.

"I'll grab a coffee," she muttered.

The moment Kim was out of earshot, Pete drew Faith closer. "Listen, when we first arrived at the scene, your ex-husband tried to tell us what happened."

All hint of tears vanished as Faith instantly turned cop. "What did he say?"

"Just the words *danger* and *keep her safe*." He hesitated, then added, "I think he was talking about you, Faith. About the fact that whoever hurt him might be after you next."

Faith pulled a notebook out of one of the many pockets of her uniform "Tell me his exact words."

Pete thought back to the scene at the edge of the parkway. The sounds of cars passing by had made it difficult to hear. *"Danger—keep her safe,"* he repeated.

"He didn't mention a name?" Faith asked.

He shook his head. "I asked, but that's when he lost consciousness."

Faith stared at him for a long moment. "Okay, listen, Pete, you'll need to tell the officers investigating the crime about what you heard. They need to know exactly what Logan said."

"I know. But what about you?" Faith might be a cop, but he didn't like the thought of her being in danger. "Do you have any idea why this happened to your ex-husband?"

"No clue," Faith admitted ruefully. "I haven't spoken to him recently. He wasn't supposed to take Jane until tomorrow."

He understood co-custody rules and nodded. "Maybe take a few days off. At least until the detectives finish their initial investigation."

Faith glanced down and put her hand on the head of the tall tan-and-black German shepherd at her side. "I'll be okay. My K-9 partner, Ricci, always has my back."

Pete wanted to press the issue, but an older cop wearing a badly fitting suit beneath a parka approached them at the same time Kim returned with her coffee. "I'm Detective Zimmerman. I need to speak to each of you, alone."

Pete glanced at Faith, who nodded. "You may want to start with the paramedics," Faith said. "They need to get back."

"I didn't hear anything," Kim protested.

"But I did," Pete added.

"Let's talk somewhere private." Zimmerman gestured to a small room off to the side.

Pete followed the detective, wondering what in the world he'd stumbled into.

Faith tore her gaze away from the handsome paramedic, dragging her attention to the issue at hand. Logan was gone. Someone had stabbed him and left him lying on the side of the road.

Why? And who exactly was in danger? Pete assumed Logan was talking about Faith, but she knew that her ex-husband had a fiancée, Claire. The woman he'd cheated on her with. The woman he'd chosen over her and their daughter.

Old news. She'd gotten over him and had grown stronger in her faith as a result.

She knew it was more likely Claire who was in danger. Maybe Claire had dragged Logan into something sketchy. Regardless, Logan was gone, leaving her little girl without a father. Faith knew she wouldn't be able to rest until his killer was brought to justice. And she'd do anything to protect Jane from harm.

"Officer Johnson?" Zimmerman's voice pulled her from her reverie. He'd finished with Pete and Kim, now it was her turn. "Are you willing to talk to me?"

It occurred to her that she could easily be a suspect. The aggrieved and divorced wife, seeking revenge. The only good news was that she'd been on duty when she heard the call over the radio about a stabbing victim named Logan Johnson. They'd found his wallet with his driver's license but no cash. She'd come to the parkway directly from the NYC K-9 Command Unit headquarters.

"Of course. I have nothing to hide." Faith glanced over to where Pete and his female counterpart stood waiting in the hallway. She tried to flash a reassuring smile.

The interview with Zimmerman was brief. Yes, she and Logan had been divorced for over a year. Yes, they shared custody of their four-year-old daughter, Jane. No, she didn't stab him. She'd been at work when she'd received the call about her ex-husband's injury. Yes, she'd come to the scene of the crime and had helped perform CPR.

It was her alibi that got her off the hook.

"I'd like my K-9 unit to help with the investigation," she said when the detective finished.

"That's not necessary," Detective Zimmerman said. "This is my jurisdiction. I'll handle it from here."

The dismissive tone of his voice put her teeth on edge. She reined in her temper, glanced down at her K-9 partner and came up with a better plan. "Fine. But I hope you'll give me updates on your progress."

"Of course," he said blithely.

She didn't believe him, but she wasn't going to sit back while this guy handled the case, either. When she was out of earshot from the detective, she called Noah Jameson, Chief of the K-9 Command Unit.

"Chief Jameson's office."

"This is Faith Johnson, I need to speak with Noah about a case I'd like some help with."

"Just a moment please." There was a pause, then Noah's deep voice could be heard. "Faith? What's going on?"

She swallowed nervously. She was the newest member of the K-9 unit and knew she might be stepping out of bounds with her request. "My ex-husband, Logan Johnson, was stabbed today and died from his wounds. The NYPD detective assigned to the case is Zimmerman, and he's refused to include me in his investigation. I'm wondering if there's a way to get cooperation between him and our K-9 unit so we can work the case together."

"As this is your ex-husband, you can't be assigned to the case," Chief Jameson pointed out.

"Maybe Brianne could take it?" She quickly named her closest friend in the unit.

There was a slight pause, before the chief responded. "Okay, I'll check her caseload."

She sighed with relief. "Thank you, sir." She ended the call, then quickly returned to the ambulance bay. She was surprised to find that Pete and Kim hadn't left, apparently waiting for her. Pete smiled. "Hey, need a ride back to your car?"

"That would be great." Faith appreciated that they'd waited. It would have been a long walk back through the snow to get her vehicle. Something she should have considered before jumping into the back of the ambulance with Ricci. But her focus had been on doing everything possible to save Logan's life.

"I'll drive," Kim offered. "We'll drop you before heading back. Our shift is almost over anyway."

Faith walked behind Pete to the ambulance. He opened the doors for her. Ricci gracefully jumped inside first and she followed. When Pete joined them, the quarters seemed more cramped than they had on the way over.

"Friend, Ricci." Faith put her hand on Pete's arm. "Friend."

Ricci sniffed at Pete for several long moments. Ricci was trained in search and rescue, and she trusted her partner's instincts more than her own.

"He's beautiful," Pete said. "Mikey wants a dog in the worst way, but I'm not sure I can handle being a single father to a four-year-old and a puppy at the same time."

She smiled ruefully. "I hear you. Ricci is well trained, and I still have trouble balancing his needs with Jane's."

Pete gazed into her eyes for a long moment until the ambulance took a turn, knocking them off balance. Faith told herself to get a grip and turned her attention to the crime scene they were approaching. Brianne would understand her desire to get a jump on the search for evidence.

She did a mental inventory of what she had in her K-9 SUV. Anything belonging to Logan?

No, but Jane's spare backpack was in there. The one that they handed off between visits. Faith hadn't touched it since she'd picked up Jane from Logan's place the previous weekend.

It might work as a scent source for Ricci.

She was so preoccupied with her thoughts that it took a moment to realize the ambulance had stopped near her SUV. Pete opened the back doors, then jumped down and offered her a hand.

She placed her gloved hand in his, feeling silly since she was perfectly capable of taking care of herself. Ricci followed.

"Thanks." Faith cleared her throat. "Guess I'll see you around the day care."

"Yeah." Pete didn't immediately leave, though. Instead he walked her to the SUV.

She opened the back passenger door, pulled out Jane's pink backpack and held it out for Ricci. "Find, Ricci."

"What are you doing?" Pete looked perplexed yet interested. "You're not going to disturb the crime scene, are you?"

"No, of course not." The uniforms who'd been called to investigate the report of an injured man on the parkway had placed crime tape around the area. "But I can search beyond it."

"I guess." Pete's expression was doubtful.

"I don't have to pick up Jane from day care until five, which gives me some time to investigate."

Pete nodded. He didn't seem anxious to get back to the ambulance, even when Kim gave the horn an impatient tap.

"Thanks for the ride." Faith tucked the backpack inside her SUV, then turned to Ricci, who was sniffing around the vehicle. He alerted right near the spot where the crime scene was, then veered along the side of the road, heading east.

Excitement surged and she praised her partner for a job well done. This must be the way Logan had come before he'd been stabbed. Had the assailant been with him, or had he gone alone? And why had her ex-husband been out here anyway? There was no abandoned vehicle nearby, forcing her to assume someone had driven Logan here, then stabbed him, before taking off.

She pulled the flashlight off her utility belt and crouched down to examine the area, searching for blood.

Nothing. Which meant Logan must have walked this way prior to being stabbed.

Ricci moved forward. She abruptly stood to follow just as the sharp echo of gunfire rang out.

"Ricci!" Faith dived toward her K-9 partner, anxious to prevent him from being injured, all too conscious of the fact that her dark uniform would be glaringly obvious against the backdrop of white snow.

TWO

"**S**top the ambulance!" Pete didn't wait for Kim to respond but opened the back of the rig and jumped out. Since the vehicle had still been moving, he tripped, fell, but tucked and rolled, somersaulting to his feet. "Faith! Are you okay?"

"Get down!" Faith's terse shout was reassuring, although he ignored her directive. Years of helping people in distress had him heading toward her in a crouched run. He reached her side in moments, noticing she had her body draped over the dog.

"Come on, let's get back inside the ambulance," he urged.

"Are you crazy? You should have stayed inside."

"Too late." He glanced around but had no clue which direction the shots had come from. "Come on, let's move."

She muttered something but there wasn't time to argue. He could see that traffic was moving around the ambulance even as Kim tried to back it toward them.

There were lots of cars around, but he knew the shot could have come from anywhere. More likely the shooter was long gone, but he understood Faith's caution.

"Let's go, then." She was on her feet, tugging at his

arm. Together with Ricci, they made a mad dash for the ambulance.

Pete made sure Faith got in first, then Ricci, before jumping in behind them.

Kim hit the gas and swerved into traffic, causing a myriad of horns to blow in protest. "You're nuts, Pete, you know that? You almost got yourself killed."

"She's right," Faith added. "You shouldn't have left the safety of the ambulance. I'm a cop, and so is Ricci. We can take care of ourselves."

He'd never jumped into the line of fire before and couldn't quite explain why he had this time, other than he couldn't bear the thought of Faith being shot while he sat doing nothing.

"Mikey needs you," Faith continued.

"I know," he finally said in his own defense. "The same way Jane needs you."

She didn't seem to have a response to that but pulled out her phone to notify Zimmerman about the recent events. After explaining about the gunfire, Faith glanced at Pete and added into the phone, "There's something else you should know, Detective." There was a pause, then she continued, "A few weeks ago, Ricci and I tracked a man who'd taken his son from his mother while in the middle of a custody dispute. We caught him, but he wasn't very happy with me, and outright threatened to get even. His name is Trevor Wilson and it could be that this attack on Logan might be related to that case. I'm not sure why he'd go after Logan, but the possibility of a connection shouldn't be ignored."

Another moment of silence as Zimmerman said something, before Faith responded, "Thanks."

Pete lifted a brow as she tucked her phone into her

pocket. "You believe this is all related to some guy named Trevor Wilson seeking revenge?"

"I have no idea. It doesn't seem likely Wilson would stab Logan, but taking shots at me? That fits." She lifted a shoulder. "I'm just trying to think of all possible angles."

"Makes sense," Pete agreed.

They fell silent for a moment as Kim put distance between them and the crime scene. "Zimmerman wasn't thrilled that I used Ricci to find Logan's scent. Wait until he finds out the K-9 unit is assisting him with the case."

"He'll get over it." Pete peered through the window. The heavy snow was replaced with light flakes that sprinkled the night. He knew that meant the temperature was dropping. The roads would grow icy soon, and he felt the need to get to the day-care center to pick up Mikey as soon as possible.

"Yeah, he will. At least he told me I didn't need to come in to give my statement, deciding our conversation was good enough."

"When we get back to the paramedic station, I'll give you a ride to pick up Jane at the day care if you like." He had given up his firefighting position to take the full-time paramedic trainer position, mostly because working normal eight-hour shifts was better for Mikey. It was one of the many changes he'd made since losing his wife, Malina, seven months ago.

She shook her head. "I need to get my police-issued SUV. I can't leave it sitting there all night."

"Isn't it part of the crime scene now?" he countered.

"Only if it was hit by one of the bullets. Besides, it's not unheard of to give cops tickets. I don't want to cause any trouble after asking my chief for a favor."

"Well, you can't go back there alone," he pointed out. "Or take Jane."

The mention of her daughter in that scenario made her wince. She blew out a breath. "Okay, fine. I'll figure something out." She glanced up at him. "Makes you wonder how long the shooter was out there."

"Yeah. Although your ex-husband was stabbed with a knife, so why use a gun now?"

"Good question." Faith's expression turned thoughtful.

Pete wasn't a cop, but he wanted to offer to protect her anyway. Which was stupid since he didn't even own a firearm, and Faith was a police officer who was comfortable carrying a gun. He gave himself a mental shake. No reason to get emotionally involved with a woman. He hadn't been a single parent for very long, and was finally settling into a rhythm. And his marriage to Malina had been rocky for several months prior to her death. He discovered he hadn't known his wife as well as he'd thought. She'd kept secrets that had put their son's life, and others, in danger.

He had no intention of heading down that path again.

Kim pulled into the space reserved for ambulances and shut down the engine. When they were all outside, Pete turned toward Faith. "Still want a lift to the day care?"

She hesitated, then nodded. "I won't have a crate for Ricci, but I don't think you'll be driving very fast in this weather, so it should be safe enough."

"I just hope we get there in time." Pete didn't like being late to pick up his son. He always felt as if the day-care workers were frowning on him for neglecting Mikey. As if he were failing at being a single father.

"Me, too."

Pete followed Kim inside, knowing that they had to restock before he could leave. Fortunately, his partner waved him off.

"I'll do it. Go pick up your son."

"Thanks, Kim. I owe you one."

She didn't answer, and he knew she hadn't forgiven him for jumping out of the ambulance to go after Faith and her K-9. Kim was younger than he was by several years. She was good, after all he'd trained her, and he couldn't blame her for not wanting to be placed in danger.

He punched out and then went back outside to find his SUV. It was covered in snow, but Faith joined him in brushing it off.

Five minutes later they were inside the car, heat blasting from the vents. Ricci was in the back, sniffing out his new environment.

"Do you think he recognizes Mikey's scent?" Pete asked as he pulled out into traffic.

"Yeah." Faith sent him a sidelong glance. "From what I hear, our kids play together all day."

He nodded, since that's what one of the day-care teachers had told him, as well. "So, uh, do you live nearby?"

"I have a small two-bedroom home that I inherited from my parents. I was going to try to sell, but that was when the market wasn't very good. So I ended up staying. I like it here."

"Me, too. And I understand making sacrifices. I changed my career and my hours for my son." He shrugged. "Whatever is best for our kids, right?"

"Right." Her tone lacked conviction and he knew she was worried about being the target of gunfire. "Maybe I will take a few days off," she added, almost as if she were talking to herself. "I can't work the weekend since Logan won't be watching Jane. Not to mention she'll need me after losing her father."

"Counseling worked for me and Mikey," he offered. Once, he wouldn't have even considered going to see a psychologist, but after Malina's passing and nearly losing his son during a kidnapping attempt, which thankfully only lasted a few hours, Pete had reconsidered his priorities.

Faith looked surprised. "I— You're probably right about that, thanks. Will you share the name of who you went to see?"

"Of course."

"I'm glad I have my church group for support, too," Faith continued. "It's bad enough to lose someone to an illness, but knowing Logan was stabbed and left for dead... I just can't understand. Why? Who would do that to him? Wilson was mad at me, but he'd have no reason to go after Logan."

Pete slowly shook his head, keeping his eyes on the snow-covered road. They were barely going fifteen miles per hour and would be late if the traffic didn't lighten up soon. "I hate to ask, but is it possible your ex was involved in something criminal?"

"No. Logan was an accountant and made a good salary. Why would he risk it for something like that?" She paused, then added, "He got engaged recently. Could be that Claire dragged him into something. But even that seems far-fetched. He had his wallet and his driver's license but no cash. Maybe a robbery, or a case of being in the wrong place at the wrong time."

"Except for the gunfire back there," he pointed out.

"Yeah."

Pete thought about how his own wife had inexplicably turned to drugs, which in turn had led to her death. He knew what it was like to live with the fact that your spouse had been murdered.

He hoped, for Faith's sake, she was right about Logan. The way he'd spoken of danger, and the gunfire that had echoed at the scene of the crime, didn't play as being a random act.

Not that it was his mystery to solve. Yet when they finally reached the day care, and both of their kids came running over to greet them, he knew deep down it wouldn't be easy to let it go.

"Mommy! You rode with Mikey's daddy?" Jane's eyes were wide in surprise, and Faith knew her daughter was far too perceptive for her own good.

"I sure did." Faith did her best to smile, but inside she couldn't bear knowing the light in her daughter's eyes would disappear when she learned her daddy was gone. Especially less than a week before Christmas. The bright Christmas lights on the artificial tree in the corner of the room mocked her. It was covered in ornaments made by the day-care kids and she could see her daughter's sparkly angel prominently displayed near the top of the tree. "Mikey's daddy will drive us home, too."

"Yay!" Mikey and Jane cried in unison, then fell into uncontrolled giggles. Faith decided she'd wait until later to tell her daughter about her father. Okay, there wasn't a good time to hear that devastating news, but for now, she wanted Jane to enjoy the thrill of riding home with her best friend.

"Can we borrow a car seat?" Pete asked the day-care worker. "I'll bring it back in the morning."

"Sure." Peggy led the way back to the supply closet. "This is exactly why we keep extras on hand."

"Thanks." He took the car seat and turned to Faith. "Ready?"

"Yes."

"Can Mikey have supper at our house?" Jane asked, as they each dressed their respective kid in snow pants, boots, jackets, hats and mittens. "Please, Mommy?"

"Oh, I don't think so." Faith risked a quick glance at

Pete, who was doing an admirable job getting Mikey bundled up for the cold. "It's late. Maybe another time, hmm?"

"Daddy, can Jane—" Mikey started, but Pete cut him off.

"No, son. Didn't you hear Mrs. Johnson? She said maybe another day."

The kids looked forlorn, but then seemed excited to be out in the snow.

"Let's make snowballs!" Mikey said as he scooped up some snow in his tiny hands.

"Okay." Jane bent down to get snow of her own.

"Don't throw it," Faith warned, as they waited for Pete to get the borrowed car seat secured.

Too late. Twin mini snowballs hit her at the same time. The kids continued giggling as they quickly scooped up more snow.

"That's enough," Pete said as he stepped away from the car.

Twin snowballs hit him, too, and he looked so exasperated, Faith had to smile. She hauled Jane into her arms before she could get any more snow and placed her in the car seat. Pete did the same with Mikey.

"We wanna have a snowball fight when we get home," Mikey announced.

"Yeah." Jane bobbed her head in agreement.

"We should have known they'd be double the trouble," Faith muttered under her breath as Pete slid behind the wheel.

"Makes you appreciate what the day-care teachers have to put up with all day, doesn't it?" He flashed a grin, and she was struck once again by how handsome he was.

Which was crazy, because she wasn't interested in a relationship. Their kids were friends for now, but she knew that would likely change over time. As soon as one of them decided the opposite gender was icky.

"Which way?" Pete asked, as he waited for the light to turn green.

"Left." She pulled her scattered thoughts together with an effort. It was impossible to imagine Logan being involved in anything criminal. He'd hated the fact that she put herself in danger on a daily basis in her quest to protect and serve. It had been one of the many issues in their marriage.

That and discovering he'd been unfaithful.

No, this had to be related to one of her cases. Trevor Wilson had threatened to seek revenge against her. Was it possible he'd found Logan and tried to get personal information from her ex? As a cop, her personal information was confidential. Was that why he'd gone after Logan rather than at her?

Different scenarios filtered through her mind as she gave Pete directions to her home. She was fortunate to have the house she'd inherited from her parents.

It was home now, and she liked that there was a small backyard for Ricci and Jane. And she was grateful she didn't have to be in a noisy apartment building.

Her lights were on timers, so she never had to bring Jane home to a dark house. Normally she was glad for that, but today, just like back at the day care, the Christmas tree visible through the living room window looked too bright and cheery in the wake of Logan's death.

"Almost home," she said to Jane.

A shadow moving past the window caught Faith's attention. She rubbed at the fog covering the inside of the window to see better. Had it been her imagination? Her mind playing tricks after the horrifying events of the day?

"What is it?" Pete asked, picking up on her change in mood.

"Probably nothing." Her voice lacked conviction. "Do me a favor and stay in the car for a minute. I'll be right back."

"Wait." Pete stopped her with his hand. "Don't go alone."

"I'll take Ricci. Not only is he a good search-and-rescue dog, but he's incredibly protective, as well." She pushed open her door. "Stay here with the kids."

Without giving him a chance to argue, she closed the door and went around to the back to let Ricci out. She didn't put him on a leash in case she needed him to help chase a perp.

She stood in the driveway for a moment, using her flashlight to illuminate the snow-covered postage-stamp-sized front yard. There were clear footprints in the snow, but more than one set, so she couldn't say for sure that they weren't the result of neighborhood kids taking a shortcut. Especially since a pair of footprints crossed the next yard to the north, as well.

Playing her light along the front window in the area where she'd caught a glimpse of the shadow, Faith looked for anything out of the ordinary. At first she didn't see anything, but then noticed a disturbance on the snow-covered edge of the windowsill.

"Come, Ricci." She put one hand on her weapon as she moved closer to the house she'd once shared with Logan. Ricci's ears were perked forward, his nose quivering as he took in the scents around them.

Stepping into the footprint marks that were already in the snow, she moved closer to the windowsill. Up close, the disturbance was even more noticeable. It appeared to her as if someone had placed their gloved hand there while leaning closer to see inside.

Kids? Maybe.

She panned the flashlight to the ground below, but again, there were too many messy boot prints to differentiate between the ones made by kids or the one made by the shadow.

Stepping from one set of footprints to the next, she went around the corner to the side window, one that also looked into the living room. Here, too, was the same indentation in the snowy edge of the windowsill. In almost exactly the same spot as the other one.

There was only one set of boot prints in the ground here, but they weren't very clear. They were large and misshapen, as if the person who'd made them had slipped in the wet snow.

Regardless, it was obvious to Faith that the intruder had leaned forward to see inside the house at both windows, using a hand on the windowsill to brace himself.

A chill that had nothing to do with the weather snaked down her back. Faith suspected that the intruder believed the lights being on meant that she was home but had quickly moved out of sight when Pete had pulled into the driveway.

She finished looking around with her flashlight but didn't find anything else remotely suspicious. No doubt the perp was long gone.

Yet just knowing that someone had been there looking through the windows put her nerves on edge. What if her theory about Trevor Wilson was right? If there was any chance Wilson had killed her ex to get personal information, like her home address, then she couldn't stay here. She absolutely could not risk her daughter's life.

Decision made, she darted toward the garage, knowing she needed to get some dog food. She quickly grabbed an old ice-cream container full of kibble, then turned and headed back to Pete's waiting SUV with Ricci at her side.

"What is it?" Pete asked through his open driver's-side window as she approached.

"Change of plan," she said with a tight smile. "I think we should let the kids have dinner together, if you don't mind a couple of houseguests."

Pete didn't hesitate. "Great idea. We'll order pizza."

"Sounds good." Faith opened the rear hatch for Ricci, then came around to climb into the passenger seat, setting the dog food on the floor.

Maybe she was being ridiculous, allowing the events of the afternoon to get to her. She'd been on the force for four years; she shouldn't let a shadow or a window-peeker scare her off.

Yet at the moment, ensuring her daughter's safety was more important than worrying about her tough-guy cop image.

Hopefully by morning, she'd know more about what happened to Logan and if his death was linked to one of her cases.

THREE

Pete wanted to ask Faith about why she'd changed her mind but knew they couldn't speak freely in front of the kids. Despite his conviction to stay single, to avoid getting into tangled relationships with women, he was secretly glad to spend more time with her.

Over the past few months, he'd done his best to create a family atmosphere for Mikey. Eva, Mikey's aunt, still came over to offer assistance, but she also recently married K-9 officer Finn Gallagher. As a result, she'd been splitting her time between helping with Mikey, training future service dog Cocoa and enjoying time with her new husband. Pete didn't blame Eva—she deserved to be happy—yet coming home to a silent house nagged at him. He wondered if Mikey noticed the emptiness, too. His son had wanted a dog from the moment he'd met Cocoa, but as the Christmas holiday approached, his son's request had become more fervent.

Eyeing Ricci in the rearview mirror, he knew that this little get-together would only renew Mikey's quest for a dog. And, really, he couldn't blame the kid.

Pete made a mental note to check out dogs at the shelter for one that would be good with kids and was already housebroken.

"I want a pepperoni pizza," Mikey announced.

"No. I want cheese," Jane argued.

He glanced at Faith with a cocked eyebrow. "Half of each kind?"

"Works for me." Faith didn't smile and seemed preoccupied with whatever had caused her to change her mind about staying at her place.

The kids continued to argue in the back seat, so he reached over to put his hand on her arm. "Are you okay? What happened?"

She shrugged and glanced back to make sure the kids weren't listening. "I saw a shadow, then found footprints in the snow beneath the front living room window. I believe someone was peering inside the house."

His gut tightened. "You should report it."

She nodded. "I will, don't worry, as soon as I find out which K-9 officer will be assigned to Logan's case. But at the moment there isn't much more to do. With this weather, everyone is short staffed. Besides, there isn't enough danger here to justify having a cop sit outside my house."

He understood her perspective. Bad weather days like today made hospitals, cops and paramedics extra busy, jumping from one disaster to the next. He was fortunate to have been able to leave work during the snowstorm. After Malina's passing, his boss had offered him a position as paramedic trainer, which enabled him to work days and pick up his son from day care.

A constant precarious balance between work and family life.

"I'll mention it to Zimmerman, too," Faith continued. "Although I have more faith in my unit than in him."

Pete hadn't been impressed with the detective, either, but kept his attention focused on the road. The Friday-evening traffic was especially horrible and it occurred to him that ordering pizza probably wouldn't work. He had frozen ones on hand, but they were all pepperoni, Mikey's favorite.

Thirty minutes later, he pulled into his driveway with a sense of relief. No sane person would voluntarily go out in this mess unless it was absolutely necessary.

"I have frozen pepperoni pizza," he told Faith. "We'll pull off some pepperoni and add more cheese for Jane."

Faith nodded. "Better than waiting for a delivery to make it through this weather."

"Yeah." He slid from the car, his feet sinking into five inches of fresh snow. He opened the back passenger seat to get Mikey out, as Faith did the same with Jane. He led the way to the front door and unlocked it. He set Mikey inside, then took Jane from Faith's arms so she could get Ricci.

He helped get the kids out of their winter gear while Faith took care of Ricci. When she came inside with the dog, the kids laughed with glee when Ricci shook the snow from his coat, spraying them with water. Faith took Ricci's K-9 vest off and hung it up to dry.

Somehow, making a meal didn't feel like a chore when he had help. He preheated the oven as Faith unwrapped the pizza, picking off pepperoni from one side and adding it to the other. The kids ran into the playroom located just around the corner from the kitchen, with Ricci hot on their heels.

Instantly the kitchen became quiet and Pete was hyperaware of Faith's presence beside him. For a moment he thought he was losing his mind because he could pick up the scent of vanilla and cranberries from her.

He cleared his throat. "How long have you been a K-9 cop?"

"Four years, although I'm relatively new to the NYC K-9 Command Unit. I transferred over to the Queens office from Manhattan about a year or so ago." She flashed a smile. "Much nicer commute, that's for sure."

"I can imagine." He leaned against the counter. "Must be awesome to work with dogs."

"I love it." She hesitated, then added, "Although, I have to say I like the investigative side of being a cop, too. Search and rescue often provides both, but the way Zimmerman ridicules my skills bothers me. Ricci was following Logan's scent when those shots were fired."

"I know." Pete remembered how things had gone down, all too clearly.

She filled a bowl of water for Ricci, then pulled out a kitchen chair and sat down. He joined her. "You would think the lead detective would ask for our assistance in a case like this. But not the old stuck-in-the-mud guys like Zimmerman."

"Listen, Faith, it might be best if you stay here for the night. You can sleep on the sofa. I'm off for the weekend, so the kids don't have to be up early." A smile tugged at the corner of his mouth. "You know they'll love having a sleepover."

"I'm not sure what to do," Faith confessed. "I need to call off work this weekend, too, now that I'm the sole parent caring for Jane. I should go to a hotel, but the idea of making you drive us there in this mess of a snowstorm seems selfish."

He didn't like the idea, either. "It's your call and I understand your concern. We don't know each other very well, except to say hi at the day-care center. But the kids will have fun. And you'll be safe. That's what matters, right?"

"Right." Her tone lacked conviction. "And I'm fairly certain we weren't followed, considering the snow."

The momentary silence was broken by the oven timer.

Pete jumped up to check the pizza. Golden-brown cheese indicated it was ready. "Tell the kids to wash up for dinner."

"Will do."

He found himself smiling as he pulled the pizza out of the oven and set it on the cardboard backing to cut it. It had been a long time since he'd shared a meal with someone— okay, a woman—and it felt nice. But then he remembered how he'd once thought the same about Malina and look where that had ended up. She'd been murdered over secrets she'd kept from him.

Once everyone was situated, the kids sitting on pillows, Faith put her hands together and looked at him. "Shall we pray?"

He shouldn't have been surprised. Earlier, Faith had mentioned getting support from her church. And his sister-in-law, Eva, was also a believer and had often prayed before meals.

Pete quickly folded his hands and stared down at them, giving Mikey a look that indicated he should follow suit. Thankfully Mikey copied Jane.

"Dear Lord, we thank You for keeping us safe in the snowstorm today. We also thank You for this food we are about to eat. We ask that you continue to guide us on Your chosen path. Amen."

"Amen," Pete echoed.

"Amen," Mikey and Jane repeated.

The rest of the meal went off without a hitch, but Pete couldn't help wondering about Faith and her beliefs about God and church.

Eva had tried to convince him to give attending church a try, but he'd resisted, his emotions too raw after learning of Malina's drug abuse and subsequent involvement in a local drug-running operation.

Yet now he thought maybe there was something he was

missing. Something that put a peaceful smile on Faith's face, despite how her ex-husband had just been murdered and she had been shot at a short while ago.

Something that might make a difference in his and Mikey's future if he had the courage to reach out and take it.

Faith could tell that praying before a meal didn't come naturally to Pete, but she was touched by the fact that he went along with it, even encouraging his son to do the same.

She hadn't dated anyone after her divorce. Between working and caring for Jane and Ricci, she didn't have the time or energy to spare. Logan hadn't been involved in the church. She'd joined shortly after moving to the NYC K-9 Command Unit because Brianne had encouraged her to attend. Two of her fellow female K-9 officers, Brianne and Lani, had welcomed her not just to the unit but as good friends. Lani had transferred to a new K-9 unit forming in Brooklyn, and Faith would miss her.

The sense of peace and rightness had cloaked her the moment she'd entered the congregation. It was refreshing to be with people who were so kind and caring. She'd instantly felt at home.

Of course, she was still learning, but feeling more confident in her faith every day. Brianne and her new husband, Gavin Sutherland, who'd be heading up the new Brooklyn K-9 unit, were both active members of the church. She'd often watched them together, thinking how wonderful it must be to have a relationship based on Christian beliefs.

"Can we play in the snow after supper?" Mikey asked.

"Yeah, can we?" Jane added.

"Not tonight, but guess what?" Faith injected enthusiasm into her tone. "We're having a sleepover! Won't that be fun?"

"A sleepover?" Mikey's eyes widened. "Yay!"

"Where will we sleep?" Jane, the ever-practical one, asked.

"You could make a tent in the playroom," Pete offered. "We'll put sleeping bags and air mattresses on the floor so it will be comfortable."

"Can Ricci sleep with us?" Mikey asked.

"Sure." At this point, Faith knew there would be no way to prevent it. Besides, Ricci was a great watchdog. "And maybe tomorrow we can play outside and make a snowman."

"Yay!" Jane shared Faith's dark hair and blue eyes, but her mouth was all Logan. Her daughter's smile reminded her of the earlier, happier days of their marriage.

Before it all fell apart.

It occurred to her that she might be using the sleepover as a way to put off telling Jane about her father's death. It was hard to know how much a four-year-old would even understand. She glanced at Pete, knowing he'd had the same conversation with Mikey several months ago.

She made a note to get more advice from him, later.

When the kids finished eating, they ran back into the playroom.

Pete began cleaning the kitchen, shooing her off when she offered to help. "I've got it."

"Okay, I'll take Ricci outside then." She put her K-9 on his leash.

Ricci took his time, sniffing all around the yard as if he'd picked up some other animal's scent. She hunched her shoulders, keeping a wary eye on the road in front of Pete's house.

The traffic had dissipated, leaving the occasional driver

passing by. Nothing looked remotely suspicious or out of place.

Faith wondered if she'd overreacted. She was here at Pete's just because of seeing the slight disturbance on the windowsills outside her home. The houses were close together; it was possible that someone had gotten an address confused. Or maybe they'd been left by kids who'd wanted to get a closer view of the Christmas tree.

A car slowly rolled down the street past Pete's house. It was difficult to figure out what kind of car it was, since it was covered in snow.

As it went by she noticed the license plate was also obscured by snow. She rested her hand on her weapon and debated calling for reinforcements. There was a flash of brake lights, as the car stopped at the intersection for what seemed like an incredibly long time.

Ricci came over, his tail thumping against her, but she kept her eyes glued to the car. There was only one person in it. Why was the car just sitting there?

Finally, the brake lights disappeared and the car turned to the right. The suspicious part of her nature made her wonder if it was going to go around the block to end up in front of Pete's house again.

She waited, holding her breath, but the car didn't return.

"Idiot," she muttered under her breath. She looked down at Ricci, who nudged her with his nose. "I'm losing it, Ricci."

Ricci wagged his tail and she hoped he wasn't agreeing with her.

After cleaning up after Ricci, she went back inside. Ricci did the shaking thing again, spraying her with water. Pete's kitchen would need to be thoroughly cleaned once they were gone. No doubt he'd had no idea what he was getting into by inviting them to stay.

Her cell phone rang, a jarring noise in the silence of the kitchen. She quickly answered it. "Hello?"

"Officer Johnson?" a deep male voice asked.

It took her a moment to recognize the detective's drawl. "Yes, this is Officer Johnson."

"This is Detective Zimmerman and I have a few more questions for you."

She sank into the kitchen chair, wondering if Chief Jameson had already reached out to assign someone from the NYC K-9 Command Unit to work with him. "I'm listening."

"Do you know Claire Munch?"

"Yes. As I told you earlier today she's engaged to my ex-husband, Logan. But I can't say I know her personally. She never said much when I dropped Jane off on the weekends she spent with her father."

"I see." There was a brief pause. "Can you be more specific? When did you last see her?"

She straightened in her seat. What was Zimmerman leading up to? "It's been at least three weeks. She wasn't always around when I'd drop Jane off."

There was another long silence as Zimmerman digested this bit of information.

"May I ask what this is about?" Faith finally asked. "Have you spoken to Claire?"

"Claire wasn't at the apartment she shared with Logan and the neighbors claim there were loud voices and some sort of argument going on between them roughly an hour before his body was found on the parkway. One of the neighbors mentioned he left, alone."

Faith felt her jaw drop. "They had an argument, and now she's missing?"

"I can't say that she's missing. For all we know she's

been staying with friends or at a hotel since their argument."

Faith's mind whirled with possibilities. Then, as long as she had Zimmerman on the phone, she asked, "Did you find any evidence of gunfire at the crime scene?"

"Nope. Nothing hit by a bullet or any bullet fragments." He paused then continued, "I looked into your guy, Trevor Wilson."

"And?"

"He was released on bail a couple of days ago. You may want to watch your back, Officer Johnson."

Released on bail? Faith couldn't believe it. "I will," she belatedly responded.

"Oh, one more thing." She waited. "Apparently your chief called mine and there's an officer from your unit who will be assigned to work with me and my partner." His tone was level, but she sensed he was frowning. "I guess you know about that."

She couldn't lie. "I asked for someone from my team to be included. I don't think you should discount the help a good K-9 cop can provide. My partner was able to track Logan's scent from the side of the road to where he'd fallen, which tells us he walked from the vehicle to the spot where he was stabbed."

"Yeah, well, that information doesn't help us much at the moment, does it?"

She wasn't going to argue the merits of her K-9 partner. "Anything else, detective?"

"That's it for now. Remember, watch your back."

She disconnected from the call and sat for a moment, ruminating on what Zimmerman had told her. Claire Munch was missing, and Trevor Wilson was out on bail.

What did it all mean?

FOUR

Pete woke up the following morning filled with an odd sense of anticipation. It had been a long time since he'd looked forward to a new day. Malina's passing, preceded by several tense weeks of marital discord, had weighed him down. He'd moved forward for Mikey's sake, and had even gone through counseling sessions with his son but hadn't experienced the simple joy of being with someone in what seemed like forever.

Excited voices coming from the first floor had him hurrying through his morning routine. When he came downstairs, the scents of coffee and maple syrup made his stomach rumble with appreciation.

"You didn't have to start breakfast," he protested as he entered the kitchen. Ricci didn't move from his seemingly new favorite spot, sitting between the two kids. He was too well trained to beg, but Pete knew he was smart enough to wait patiently for a morsel of food.

"Actually I did." Faith gave him a harried look. She'd borrowed his sweats to sleep in last night and hadn't changed back into her uniform yet. She looked adorable wearing his oversize things. "The kids were up early and complaining of being hungry so it was either listen to them whine or cook. I decided to make myself at home in your kitchen."

"Sorry about that." Pete realized he'd slept much better than his houseguest. "I can take it from here."

She waved the spatula at him dismissively. "Don't be silly. I'm already on the second batch of pancakes. Sit down. These will be ready shortly."

After filling a mug with coffee, he did as she suggested. Mikey and Jane were seated on their pillows and had sticky smears of syrup on their faces. Mikey was blond, like Malina had been, and Jane was dark, like her mother, but at the moment they were acting like siblings. One minute they were arguing, the next they were grinning at each other.

"Daddy, can we build a snowman after breakfast?" Mikey asked.

"Yeah, can we?" Jane echoed.

Since Faith had pretty much promised they could, he exchanged a glance with her before granting permission. "Sure."

"You'll have to wait until we eat, too," Faith cautioned. "You can use that time to clean up the mess from your fort."

"I don't wanna clean," Mikey protested.

"Me, either," Jane chimed in.

"Then I guess you don't want to go outside to build a snowman." Faith flipped the pancakes on the griddle.

Pete hid a smile as the two kids looked at each other, then back at their mostly empty plates.

"Okay," Jane said. "We'll clean up our fort."

"Yeah," Mikey agreed.

"Glad to hear it." Faith took a damp washcloth to both kids' hands and faces, before lifting them off their seats and onto the floor. Ricci gamely followed them into the playroom.

"That was slick." Pete stood and brought the empty serving plate to the counter so she could fill it with fresh pancakes. "I should take lessons from you."

"Trust me, it's trial and error every day," she said in a wry tone. She added pancakes and joined him at the table. "It's not easy being a single parent, is it?"

"Not one bit." He forked two pancakes onto his plate then looked at her expectantly. "I, uh, suppose you'd like to pray?"

Faith nodded and bowed her head. "Dear Lord, we thank You for this food we are about to eat. We also ask for Your strength and guidance as we seek Your chosen path. Amen."

"Amen." Pete looked at her curiously. "You really believe God has a chosen path for us?"

"Absolutely." Faith didn't hesitate. "It helps me get through each day knowing God is watching over me and Jane."

Pete frowned for a moment, staring blindly down at his food. "It's hard for me to believe that God wanted Mikey to lose his mother and for Jane to lose her father. It doesn't seem right that he would put young, innocent children through something like this."

"I know it's not always easy to understand God's plan," Faith admitted. She reached out to touch his forearm for a moment, heat radiating from her fingertips, before taking another bite of her pancake. "And it's true God often works in mysterious ways. I don't have all the answers. All we can do is lean on Him for strength while moving forward, trusting that we will understand his plan for us when it's time."

He didn't find Faith's answer particularly helpful, but he decided to let it go for now. The food was delicious, and he found himself more hungry than he'd been in a long time.

"You cooked, so I'll clean up," he announced, picking up his empty plate and carrying it to the sink. "After I check on the kids."

Pete headed into the playroom to find the kids playing with toys rather than cleaning up. "Mikey, put the blanket away. Jane, please put the pillows away. When that's finished, you can go back to your playing."

"Oh, Dad," Mikey huffed, but did as directed.

Pete turned and found Faith behind him. She was looking at two framed drawings on the wall. One was a picture Mikey had done at the day-care center and had given him for Father's Day. It depicted their family—father, mother and Mikey. The family Mikey had lost. The other was a drawing Pete had done with colored pencils, depicting himself, Malina and Mikey in a replica of his son's.

"Did you do this?" Faith asked pointing to his drawing. "It's amazing."

He nodded. "I wanted a way for Mikey to remember his mom."

"You've very talented." Faith glanced up at him in awe.

"Thanks." He wasn't, but it was nice of her to say so. He went into the kitchen to start the dishes, and Faith joined him at the sink.

It was nice to have someone to share the chore with. Ten minutes later they were bundling up the kids to head outside. Mikey and Jane were beyond excited to jump into the newly fallen snow, giggling madly as they tossed snowballs at each other.

Ricci joined the fun, playing in the snow along with the kids. With his vest off, Ricci knew he wasn't working. When they'd made a rather lopsided snowman, Faith took a step back to admire their work. "All we need is the face."

"I have carrots inside, for the nose." Pete thought about what was in his fridge. "I'm sure I can find something for the eyes, too."

"He needs a mouth, too, Daddy!" Mikey said with excitement.

Pete managed to find everything they needed. He returned a few minutes later. "Dark chocolate for the eyes," he said as he pressed them into the small snowball of the head. "Candy canes for the mouth." He pushed those into the snow, as well. He handed the large carrot to Faith. "Last but not least, the nose."

Faith took the carrot, but as she was about to stick it in, Ricci jumped up to grab it. Faith tried to hold it out of the dog's reach but fell backward into the snow.

"Ricci, no!" Jane cried, but it was too late. Ricci had the carrot in his mouth and began galloping around the yard, unwilling to let it go.

The kids ran after Ricci, who obviously thought this was a fun game. Pete offered a hand to Faith.

"Thanks," she murmured as he helped her to her feet.

He stared down at her smiling face, fighting the insane urge to kiss her. Instead, he released her hand and stepped back in an attempt to break the sudden awareness between them.

They were both single parents. Both had four-year-old children. His wife had been murdered and so had Faith's ex-husband. But that was where the similarities between them stopped.

He couldn't risk going down this path again. There could be nothing more than friendship between them.

Faith couldn't believe she'd nearly kissed Pete. She hadn't been interested in men since her divorce and had no intention of acting on any sort of attraction now.

Despite her chief's directive, she had a murderer to find. And a daughter to keep safe. Neither of those priorities involved Pete Stallings.

"I'm cold," Jane said.

"Me, too," Mikey added.

"I'm not surprised. You're both wet and covered in snow. Let's go inside." Faith glanced at Pete. "It's time for us to head home."

"I'm happy to take you wherever you need to go," Pete answered. They went into the kitchen and shucked their wet things. "Maybe we should throw the kids' coats, hats and mittens in the dryer before heading back out."

She wanted to hit the road but saw the wisdom of his suggestion. "Okay."

Pete disappeared with his arms full of clothes. The kids ran into the playroom, with Ricci on their heels. Her phone rang from an unfamiliar number and she hesitated a moment before answering. "Officer Johnson."

At first, there was nothing but heavy breathing on the other end of the line. Faith tightened her grip on the phone. "Who is this?"

"I'm watching you."

A chill snaked down her spine and she quickly glanced over her shoulder. The voice was mechanical, difficult to tell if it was from a man or a woman, but she thought this was something Trevor might do. But how had he gotten her number? "What is your name?"

More silence.

"I'll find out who you are," she said in a stern voice.

The call abruptly ended. She called the number back, but it didn't go through. The caller must have turned the phone off. She stared at the screen for a moment, knowing she'd have to find out who the number belonged to as soon as she was back at headquarters.

I'm watching you.

She didn't like it but tried to shake off the sense of forbidding. As she returned to the kitchen, her phone rang for a second time, but she relaxed as she recognized Brianne's number. "Hey, how are you?" Thankfully Pete was still down in the basement, where she assumed the laundry facilities were located.

"I'm fine, but the real question is—how are you?" Brianne's voice held a note of concern. "The chief asked me to help work the case involving your ex-husband. I'm sorry, Faith."

"It's terrible," she agreed, eyeing her daughter. Faith felt bad that she hadn't told Jane the news about her father, yet. "Have you spoken to Detective Zimmerman?"

"Yes." Brianne's tone indicated she wasn't impressed. "He's annoyed that he has to work with us. He claims that Logan's fiancée is missing."

"I heard." Faith hesitated before continuing, "I think we should use Ricci or one of the other K-9s to pick up her scent."

"Interesting idea," Brianne said thoughtfully. "But don't you think she probably left by car?"

"Maybe, but it's worth a shot. I'm worried that Claire got mixed up with something criminal and dragged Logan into the middle of it."

"We can't forget about Trevor Wilson, either," Brianne pointed out. "He's out on bail, but I haven't been able to get a line on him."

"Could be he skipped town." Faith didn't really believe it. She glanced over as Pete came into the kitchen to refill his coffee mug. "Listen, I'm going to pick up my vehicle. Has it been towed?"

"Unfortunately, yes. We were put on notice that it's in the tow lot not far from headquarters."

"Great, just great." Faith hoped Chief Jameson wouldn't hold the towing against her. "Thanks, Brianne. I also found footprints in the snow outside my windows last night.

Could be neighborhood kids, but the timing is suspicious. I have some other thoughts on how to proceed with our investigation."

"Our investigation?" her friend echoed. "Chief Jameson asked me to take it since you're too close to remain objective."

"And I'm sure Chief Jameson knew full well that I wasn't going to sit idly by while you and Zimmerman did all the work. He and his siblings worked hard on their oldest brother's murder, didn't they? And they solved the crime."

"Yes, they did." Brianne was silent for a moment and Faith could feel Pete's gaze boring into her from across the kitchen. "Okay, fine. We'll discuss strategy. We can meet at the Command Unit."

"Sounds good. Thanks, Brianne." Faith disconnected the call and pushed the phone into her pocket.

Pete eyed her over the rim of his mug. "We should be ready to go in twenty minutes."

"Thanks." She didn't really want to leave but knew she couldn't put off telling Jane about her father forever. And she would, tonight. "You mentioned taking Mikey to a therapist. What's her name and number?"

Pete set his coffee aside and quickly scrolled through his phone for the information. He wrote it down and handed it to her. "I added my number, too, in case you need to call me."

She blushed and then quickly jotted her number for him, as well.

"When are you going to tell Jane?"

"I don't know." The upcoming conversation loomed overhead like a thundercloud. "Soon. Tonight."

He nodded, his dark eyes serious.

"I'm glad she's been focused on playing with Mikey."

The corner of Pete's mouth tipped up in a smile. "They are something, aren't they?"

"For sure." There it was again, that strange awareness shimmering between them. She cleared her throat. "I'm going to take Ricci out for a bit."

Fifteen minutes later, when Faith came back with the dog, Pete had the kids bundled up in their warm clothes. They piled into his vehicle, each parent getting their respective child secured in their safety seat.

"Where to?" Pete asked as he slid behind the wheel.

She gave him the address of the NYC K-9 Command Unit. "The tow lot is a couple of blocks down from there and that's where I need to pick up my vehicle before I meet with Brianne."

Pete nodded and kept his attention on the road. "Are you going to have someone check out your house?"

"Ricci and I can do it." She felt foolish for the way she'd overreacted the night before. She was a cop and could protect herself. It was Jane who made her feel vulnerable.

"Maybe you could ask Brianne to stay with you for the night, just to be sure." Pete's gaze was serious. "For Jane's sake if nothing else."

"I will." She tried to smile. "Thanks for everything."

"My pleasure."

His words made her heart thump wildly in her chest. She kept her gaze out the window and listened to the kids playing I Spy in the back seat.

"Take a right at the next corner. The tow lot is another block down the street on the left."

He did as she asked, pulling up a few minutes later in front of the tow lot. "Give me a minute, okay?"

"Sure." He kept the car running to keep the kids warm.

Faith slid out from the passenger seat and hurried up to

the shack-like building. The owner of the lot ran her credit card, then gestured toward the back. "It's over there."

"Thanks." Keys in hand, she approached the white police SUV with the K-9 logo.

Shivering a bit, she made her way toward her car, stopping short when she saw the broken rear passenger-side window. She glanced around warily, then approached the vehicle.

She peered inside. It seemed undisturbed. The only thing she noticed was that Jane's pink backpack was gone. She distinctly remembered placing it back in the SUV after using it for Ricci to pick up Logan's scent.

She spun around and stalked back to the owner, rapping on the shack's door frame to get his attention. "Hey!"

"What?" He sounded cranky.

"There's a big hole in the side window of my vehicle."

"That was there when we picked it up." He thrust a piece of paper at her. She read the scrawl, taking note of the broken window. "I keep cameras on my lot. That didn't happen here."

Faith turned to look back at her car. Was the damage the result of kids acting up?

Or something more sinister?

And why on earth would anyone take Jane's backpack?

Faith thought fast as she returned to Pete's vehicle. He looked surprised when she gestured for him to roll down his window. "Hey, will you keep Jane with you for a while longer?"

"Of course, but what's going on?"

"My vehicle has a broken window and I don't want to drive around with it open—it will be too cold for Jane. I need to meet with Brianne anyway. She'll drive me home for my personal SUV and I'll pick up Jane when I'm finished."

He slowly nodded. "Okay, no problem. Do you need a ride?"

"No, I'll walk to headquarters. It's not far. Will you open the back hatch so I can get Ricci?"

He hit the button so she could let her K-9 partner out. The German shepherd sniffed the air, then took his position at her left side. She closed the back, then returned to the driver's side of the vehicle. "Thanks again, Pete. You're awesome to do this for me."

"That's what friends are for." He smiled. "I'm going to take the kids to Griffin's for lunch. Why don't you head over when you're finished?"

Spending additional time with him was a bad idea but she quickly nodded. At least this way, she wouldn't have to bother Brianne for a ride back to her place. "Okay."

After waiting for him to drive off, she and Ricci took a shortcut through the buildings toward the street. At the corner, she was about to cross on the green walk signal when a gunshot echoed loudly.

"Ricci, down!" Faith dropped to the ground, covering her partner with her body, mentally bracing for the impact of a bullet when she heard a second shot.

FIVE

Pete heard the gunfire and instinctively slammed on his brakes. A horn blared from behind him, and he realized stopping was putting the kids in danger.

He couldn't turn around in an attempt to find Faith, no matter how much he wanted to.

He kept going until he could safely pull over. Grabbing his phone, he called 911 and was informed they were already aware of the gunfire. Next he called Faith's cell, but even after endless ringing, she didn't pick up.

Despite knowing help was on the way, his chest tightened with worry.

For the first time in years, he found himself praying that God was watching over Faith and Ricci.

"Where's Mommy?" Jane asked, her voice trembling.

"She'll join us in a little while." He purposefully kept the timeframe vague even as his heart thudded painfully in his chest.

He didn't want to believe Faith was in trouble, but if that was the case, why hadn't she answered her phone?

He tried again. Still no response.

Gripping the steering wheel tightly, he debated where to go. It went against the grain to leave Faith and Ricci back there, but what other option did he have?

What would Faith want him to do?

Protect Jane as if she were his own child.

Okay, then that was exactly what he intended to do.

He'd take the kids to Griffin's and wait for her there.

Faith remained hunched over Ricci for what seemed like forever until the cops arrived. She was thankful the pedestrians had scattered when they'd heard the shots, two close together.

She finally stood and glanced around, confirming no one appeared hurt. Whoever had used the gun wasn't a good marksman.

Did Trevor Wilson know how to use a gun? She wished she knew.

"You're a good boy," she praised Ricci as the patrol officers secured the area. This was the second time someone had taken shots at her and Ricci, and she didn't like it.

Within moments Brianne Sutherland and her K-9, Stella, rushed over from headquarters. "Are you okay? What happened?"

"Another attempt to get rid of me and Ricci." Faith felt her phone vibrate in her pocket but ignored it. "Did you see anything unusual?"

"No." Brianne frowned. "Clearly the same person who stabbed your ex-husband is after you now, too."

No argument there. "When I'm finished giving my statement to Zimmerman, who should be here soon, I wanted to ask about the possibility of going to Logan's to search for Claire's scent."

"I went with Finn Gallagher earlier today. His K-9 partner, Abernathy, tracked Claire's scent from the house to the driveway, but then lost it."

Faith felt her shoulders slump. "Find anything else at the house?"

"A broken glass in the kitchen, but no other indication of a struggle." Brianne handed her a red blouse sealed in an evidence bag. "I brought this along, in case you need it for something else. It's Claire's and worked well as a scent source for Abernathy."

"Thanks." Faith took the bag, stifling a flash of disappointment. "I have a cell number to track down, from a crank caller, and now this." She waved her hand at the crime scene. "Sooner or later we're going to find the evidence we need to identify the jerk behind these attacks."

Before Brianne could say anything in response, Detective Zimmerman arrived, looking as grouchy as usual. After parking his car, he strolled toward her. "Officer Johnson. I understand someone took another shot at you?"

"Yes. And I'm ready to give my statement." She would remain professional with this guy if it killed her.

"Let's have it."

Faith went through the events of the past hour, starting with the crank call, then adding the damage to her police vehicle and ending with the gunfire. Zimmerman didn't take many notes and seemed only interested in the damage to her car and the gunfire.

"Two shots?" he asked.

"Yes." She thought back. "There was a pause between them, different from what you would usually hear from a semiautomatic weapon."

"I see. And who knew you'd be here today?"

She frowned. He had a point. If she and Pete hadn't been followed, who would know she was here? Granted she was within a block of headquarters, but still. Could this be a coincidence? No way. She didn't believe that for a nanosecond. "No one other than Pete Stallings and Brianne Sutherland."

"I was at the K-9 Command Unit when the shots were fired," Brianne added.

"And Pete is with our respective kids," she added. "He was heading for Griffin's."

"Any idea which direction the shots came from?" Zimmerman pressed.

Faith swallowed hard, feeling like a failure. It had all happened so quickly, but she was a trained cop. She should have paid closer attention. "I can't say for sure, but my gut reaction was that the threat came from the north."

Zimmerman's gaze was skeptical, but he didn't say anything more. When he turned to leave, she stopped him.

"Wait. What's the word on Trevor Wilson and Claire Munch?"

A flash of annoyance crossed his face. "Nothing yet. But we'll find them."

"Do you have Wilson's phone number? I'd like to see if it matches the crank call I received earlier today." She tucked the evidence bag under her arm and pulled out her phone. There were several missed calls from Pete.

He must have heard the gunfire and called to check on her. She hoped the kids were safe.

Zimmerman pulled out his notebook and recited a number. It didn't match the call. "What about Claire's number?"

He told her that one, too, and it didn't match, either. She hadn't really thought it would. Zimmerman said he'd be in touch and walked away.

Frankly, the top suspect on her list was Trevor Wilson, the perp who'd vowed to seek revenge. Who else would risk shooting at a cop? But Jane's missing backpack nagged at her. Why had it been taken? Simply because she'd used it to track Logan's scent? Had Wilson been hiding out there at the crime scene, watching her? Had he staked out their Command Unit to find her here today? Had he been watching as she'd checked out her damaged car?

Too many questions without answers, yet Wilson stealing the backpack was the only thing that made sense.

Was Pete's house safe? None of the attempts against her had taken place there, but it could be just a matter of time.

Something to think about.

"Listen, Faith, I need to go." Brianne's voice drew her from her dark thoughts.

"So soon? What about our plan to discuss strategy?"

Brianne held up her phone. "Bomb threat has just been called in. Stella and I are up. I'll check in with you later, okay?"

"Sure." Faith understood duty had to come first. After Brianne left, she called Pete.

"Faith? I heard the gunfire as we were leaving. Are you all right?" His tone was low and frantic with concern.

"I'm fine. Sorry I couldn't call you back sooner."

"I was worried," he admitted.

"I know. Are you at Griffin's with the kids?"

"Yeah, I figured that's what you'd want me to do."

"Exactly what I wanted you to do, thanks." She hesitated, then added, "I want you to understand how much it helped me to know Jane was safe with you and Mikey."

"I'm glad." His voice was soft and strangely intimate. She hadn't really depended on a man in a very long time. And it felt nice to have Pete's support. "Although I'm not going to lie. I wanted to come back to find you, to make sure you were all right. Driving away wasn't easy."

Her heart softened in her chest at his words. "That's nice, but you did the right thing in keeping the kids safe."

There was a brief silence before Pete continued. "Are you still going to come meet us? Jane is asking for you."

She squelched a pang of guilt. "Soon. I need my laptop

computer from headquarters, then can head over to Griffin's. I hate to bother you again, but it looks like I'll need a ride back to my place to pick up my SUV."

"Not a problem. I'll keep the kids occupied until you get here." Was there a hint of satisfaction in his voice? Or was it her imagination?

Ridiculous to think he was eager to see her. More likely, he was getting tired of being on kid duty. Even though Jane and Mikey got along really well, they still argued the way only four-year-olds could.

"See you soon," Pete said.

She found herself smiling as she disconnected. What was wrong with her? She and Ricci had been shot at for the second time. That was far more important than her strange feelings toward Pete. She told herself to focus and tightened Ricci's leash. "Ready to get out of here?"

Ricci's brown eyes seemed to say yes.

Griffin's was located just a couple of blocks away, in the opposite direction from the scene of the crime, but one of the local beat cops agreed to drive her and Ricci over so they didn't have to walk. An extra precaution since there was no way of knowing if the gunman was still hanging around.

"Would you mind stopping at headquarters so I can get my laptop?" she asked the patrol officer.

"Sure thing." He pulled over and double-parked in front of the building.

"I'll be less than five minutes," she assured him. She jumped out of the car, with Ricci at her side, and hurried in. At least with her work computer she could trace the phone number, and maybe continue working the case, too.

Most of the desks were empty because they were typically short staffed on the weekends, especially before the holiday. Faith headed to her cubicle. She set the evidence bag on the corner of the desk and quickly reached for her laptop computer and power cord. She stuffed them in a carrying case, added the evidence bag and then took up Ricci's leash.

The patrol officer was waiting for her. She let Ricci into the back seat first, then slid in beside him. "Thanks."

"Now to Griffin's, right?" He met her gaze in the rear-view mirror.

"Please."

He dropped her and Ricci off in front of the main entrance. Griffin's was known as a K-9 cop hangout; the new owner was a former K-9 officer and there was a special walled-in patio area where four-legged friends were welcome. Above the door frame were the words: *The Doghouse— Home to NYC's Finest.*

A cheerful hostess greeted her and quickly led her to the patio area, where Pete and the kids were waiting. The patio was fairly warm thanks to the portable heaters that had been installed to keep it open year-round.

"Hey." Pete jumped to his feet, greeting her with a warm smile.

Walking toward him and giving him a quick hug seemed like the natural thing to do. The musky male scent of him enveloped her, but she didn't linger before crossing over to give Jane a quick kiss. "Were you good for Mr. Pete?"

"Yes, Mommy." Jane bobbed her head earnestly. "Me and Mikey didn't fight at all."

"Yes, we were very good," Mikey added.

Pete coughed in a way that told her the kids were stretching the truth. But she smiled as she sat down, hanging the computer bag over the back of her chair.

"I'm glad to hear it."

"We didn't order yet—we wanted to wait for you." Pete glanced up at her from the menu. "The kids were good about waiting, they've been coloring place mats and playing Tic Tac Toe."

"That was nice." She knew the menu well, so it didn't take time for her to decide. Their server came to take their orders, then quickly disappeared toward the kitchen area.

While the kids were busy coloring on their paper place mats, she gave Pete a quick overview. "Two shots, but no damage from what I could tell. They're still looking for evidence that may have been left behind by the perp."

Pete's expression was grim. "I'm glad you and Ricci are okay."

"Me, too."

"Are you sure you won't come back to my place?" His gaze was serious. "I feel like we should stick together."

It was tempting, but she figured the kids could use a break. "Maybe another time."

This time, she could see the flash of disappointment in his eyes.

Their food didn't take long, and soon the conversation grew silent as they enjoyed their meal. Once the kids were finished eating, they began to bicker back and forth until Pete grabbed new place mats for them to color.

When the server dropped off their check, Pete pounced on it before she could blink. "Wait, what do I owe?"

"I've got it." Pete waved her away.

"No, really, you've done more than enough for us."

"It's the least I can do, considering what you've been through." Tiny lines furrowed his brow. "I know you're a trained cop and have Ricci as your partner, but please be careful. I don't like what's going on around you."

"I will." She was touched by his concern. Pete's attitude toward her job was different from Logan's. Her ex had always acted as if he had something to prove. As if her being a cop somehow lessened his masculinity. He'd been an avid outdoorsman, bragging that he could shoot a gun as accurately as she could.

As if that had mattered.

What Logan hadn't seemed to understand was that no cop wanted to fire his or her weapon in the line of duty. Not just because of the endless paperwork.

A cop's mission was to protect and serve. She'd joined the NYC K-9 Command Unit, pairing with a search-and-rescue dog, just because it was less likely she'd have to fire her weapon. Not that she couldn't—she would do whatever necessary to arrest the bad guys—but it wasn't some sort of notch on a cop's belt.

She gave herself a mental shake. Why all these memories about Logan? He was gone and she should be thinking of how she would tell Jane the devastating news. As soon as they got home, she'd tell her daughter the truth.

"Ready?" Pete asked, rising to his feet.

"Yes." She reached for Jane's coat, then drew on her own, looping the computer bag over her shoulder.

Five minutes later, they were back outside, walking to Pete's car. There were still several squads in the area, but she kept a keen eye out for anything amiss as they approached Pete's vehicle.

It was more than likely the shooter was long gone by now, but she didn't rest easy until they were several miles away.

The kids went back to playing I Spy as Pete drove to Forest Hills. She briefly considered Pete's offer to have them stay another night, but then dismissed it.

She couldn't put off telling Jane about her father much longer. Besides, she felt certain she and Jane would be safe at home. The footprints were likely from kids. She was armed and had Ricci.

So far, the two shooting attacks had taken place from

afar and not with any great accuracy. She had the impression that Trevor Wilson didn't want to get too close, knowing Ricci was protecting her.

"Aw, Mom," Jane protested when Pete pulled into their driveway. "I want to play with Mikey more."

"Yeah, we wanna play," Mikey chimed in.

"I'm sure you'll see each other again soon." Faith glanced at Pete's handsome profile. "We're attending church in the morning if you're interested in joining us."

He looked surprised at her offer and shrugged. "Maybe, we'll see."

She was disappointed but didn't let it show and told herself not to push. "I'm going to take Ricci out first. Will you give me a few minutes?"

He nodded.

Faith jumped down, then let Ricci out from the back. She clipped on his leash and had only taken two steps when Ricci began to growl low in his throat.

"What is it, boy?" A quick glance at her house didn't give any reason for alarm. Still, she trusted her K-9's instincts more than her own, so she pulled her weapon and held it at the ready as she approached her home.

Ricci's growls grew louder, and she came to an abrupt stop when she noticed the door wasn't closed all the way.

Her K-9 partner didn't give the signal for an intruder, but he continued to growl as she cautiously approached the house. Ricci's nose twitched and quivered as he took in the strange scent. The German shepherd's specialty was search and rescue, but he was also incredibly protective.

If there was someone inside, Ricci would let her know. But he didn't let out the three sharp staccato barks the way he was trained to do. Instead, the low growling continued.

With Ricci at her side, she gave the door a quick push, staying back for a moment before entering the dwelling.

She rushed over the threshold, then stood with her back pressed against the wall as she swept her gaze around the kitchen and living area.

The place was a mess. She sucked in a harsh breath as she digested the extent of the damage. Her home had been completely and thoroughly ransacked. But why? And how? It appeared the perp had used a key.

Ricci's growls grew louder as he dropped his nose to the floor, picking up the scent of the intruder. He strained at the leash, so she gave him more lead. If anyone was hiding inside, he'd give the signal.

Her K-9 led the way, moving back and forth in a jerky path, from one room to the next, continually growling at the strange scent. But eventually he returned to her side, gazing up at her with expectant eyes, as if waiting for her next command.

Ricci's actions made it clear the intruder was long gone, leaving a destructive, almost vindictive mess behind.

SIX

Pete knew something was wrong the moment Faith pulled out her weapon. He waited for what seemed like eons, phone in hand, ready to call 911 the moment he heard the sound of gunfire.

But all remained quiet. Too quiet.

When Faith returned to the vehicle a few moments later, she stayed outside with Ricci, so he lowered the passenger-side window so they could talk.

"What happened?"

She glanced back at the kids before answering. "It's been ransacked," she said carefully. "I need to call Zimmerman."

Ransacked? Trouble had continued to follow Faith over the past twenty-four hours, making it clear that Logan's last whispered warning about danger was directed toward his ex-wife.

It gave Pete a chill to think about how Logan must have spoken with his attacker. Had it been that Trevor Wilson guy she'd mentioned? Had he bragged that Faith would be next as he stabbed Logan?

All for revenge?

Faith stepped back from the car to make her calls. He could hear her updating both Detective Zimmerman and

Brianne about the most recent problem. He heard her make a third call, to Finn Gallagher. He knew that Finn's yellow lab, Abernathy, was trained in tracking scents, the same way Ricci was.

"Pete, will you please take the kids back to your place?" Faith asked when she finished. "I'm going to stay here with Ricci until the scene has been processed. When we're finished, I'll come to pick up Jane using my personal SUV."

It went against his nature to leave her here alone, even knowing the police were on their way. The last time he'd done that, someone had shot at her. But he understood the kids needed to stay safe, and he had faith in Ricci. "Okay, but I think you should pack a couple of bags. You and Jane can't stay here."

"I know." She blew out a heavy breath. "I'll see if I can find a dog-friendly hotel."

"This close to Christmas?" Pete didn't try to hide his skeptical tone. "The offer to stay with me still stands."

"Thanks." Her smile didn't reach her eyes. Whatever she'd seen inside continued to bother her. "But you'll get tired of having houseguests eventually."

Regular houseguests, maybe, but not Faith. It made him uneasy to realize how quickly he'd grown accustomed to having her around. "Whatever you decide is fine. Just know the offer stands."

"I appreciate that." She turned to glance over her shoulder at her home for a moment, before facing him. "You know, it really upsets me to have this happen right before Christmas."

"Maybe that's exactly what Wilson is aiming for."

She slanted him a thoughtful look. "You could be right about that. He clearly wants revenge against me, shooting at me twice and now this. Maybe ruining the holiday is extra icing on the cake."

The guy had to be mentally unbalanced, but Pete kept the thought to himself. The kids were still playing I Spy and thankfully weren't paying any attention to the adult conversation.

"Climb in," he invited. "I'll stick around until the cops arrive."

"No need." Faith stood with one hand on her gun, the other resting on the top of Ricci's head. "We're good here. But I'm not sure how long it will take us to finish up. Could be late, though. I know we had a late lunch, but you may have to feed the kids dinner, too."

"Mikey has to eat—what's one more?" He really wished he'd gone grocery shopping. "Don't worry. I'll think of something."

"Thanks, Pete." Faith's gaze turned serious. "For everything."

"You're welcome." He wished that he could offer her a comforting hug, but of course that was impossible. And why was he so keenly aware of the attraction he felt toward her?

She smiled, then stepped back, gesturing for him to get going. He didn't want to leave but raised the window and put the vehicle in Reverse.

After he backed out of the driveway, he took note of a dark-colored sedan rolling down the road toward Faith's house. He tightened his grip on the steering wheel, until he noticed the flashing red light on the dash.

Zimmerman. Pete pulled over to the side of the road, watching as the sedan entered Faith's driveway. Only when he recognized the balding rotund detective did he merge into traffic.

"I want my mommy." Jane sounded as if she might cry at any moment.

"She's meeting us soon," Pete assured the little girl. "I

promise. In the meantime, we'll have fun playing together. We can make another fort if you'd like."

Jane considered this for a moment before relenting. "Okay."

Pete realized how much he felt like a husband planning the afternoon while anxiously waiting for his spouse to return home.

And the idea was more appealing than it ought to have been.

Zimmerman asked if anything was missing, which reminded Faith of the pink backpack that had been taken from the police SUV.

She told him about that, but then gestured wearily at the mess. "It will take me a while to go through everything to see if anything was taken, but the TV and my personal laptop computer are still here, so that tells you robbery wasn't the motive. Other than that, I don't have many valuables. My jewelry box was the first thing I checked."

"What jewelry is missing?" Zimmerman asked.

"Nothing. I had a pair of gold earrings and matching bracelet left to me by my mother, and a pearl necklace, which are still there." She shook her head helplessly. "It doesn't make any sense. If you're going to get inside to tear the place up, why not at least try to make it look like a robbery?"

"It looks vindictive to me," Zimmerman muttered.

For the first time, she agreed with his assessment. Christmas ornaments were broken, sofa cushions tossed around. But the greatest damage was to her bedroom.

Jane's had been tossed, too, but not with the same vengeance.

"How did the perp get inside?" Zimmerman asked.

She'd been trying to figure that out for herself. "The

lock is still intact, although whoever did this didn't bother to relock it on their way out. Either someone is an expert at picking locks, including the dead bolt, or they had a key." She'd already called the locksmith to have the locks changed.

"But how would someone get a key?"

"The only thing I can think of is that there may have been a key ring inside the missing backpack. Logan and I didn't normally keep our keys there, it's filled with stuff Jane might need while staying at each other's homes, but maybe for some reason, he tucked a spare set inside."

Zimmerman nodded thoughtfully, sweeping a gaze over the shambles. "Could be someone was searching for a specific item."

"Like what?" The mess did look vindictive, which made her think once again of Trevor Wilson and his vow to seek revenge. "I'm not sure it matters at this point, since I can't say for sure anything is even missing. But I'll let you know if I come up with anything."

"See that you do." Zimmerman turned and headed toward the door. He hesitated, then looked back at her. "Your K-9 friends checked out Claire's house but didn't find anything useful."

Was that a dig against the NYC K-9 Command Unit? "And what have you come up with? Have you located Claire or Trevor Wilson?"

Zimmerman flushed. "Not yet, but we will. I've issued a BOLO for Wilson. He can't hide forever."

She knew that when a *Be On the Lookout* was issued that every squad in the vicinity would have Wilson's picture up in the corner of their computer screen. It was somewhat reassuring.

"What about Claire?"

Zimmerman shrugged. "She's a person of interest but

could also be another victim. We've left messages for her mother and sister but haven't heard back yet. We plan on taking a ride upstate to check on them, soon. In the meantime, you'll want to continue watching your back. All the animosity is directed toward you at the moment."

"I will." In her opinion, Zimmerman should issue a BOLO for Claire, too, but Faith kept her thoughts to herself. Because she couldn't deny he was right about the perp coming after her.

First Logan, then the two episodes of gunfire, the smashed window of her vehicle and now this.

What was next? If this was Trevor's work, she knew there would be another attempt to harm her.

It made her consider the possibility of having Jane spend the night with Mikey, leaving her to go to a hotel with Ricci. At least that way, the danger would likely stay focused on her. Then again, she'd feel better staying close to Jane.

Once the officers had left and the locksmith had changed the locks, she surveyed the mess with a sense of despair. She took the time to put Jane's room back in order and straightened up the living room. At least half the ornaments on the tree were broken, so she cleaned up all the broken glass to protect Ricci and Jane.

But as darkness fell, she sat at the kitchen table, with Ricci at her side, and used her phone to find the nearest hotels.

There were some hotels with vacancies, but they were all located in Manhattan and not only were they above her price range, they didn't seem dog friendly.

She stared down at her phone for a long moment. Was she looking for a good reason to stay with Pete again? The sofa hadn't been too bad; the only downside was that the kids had woken her early with their giggling.

The memory made her smile. "Guess we're going back, Ricci," she murmured to her partner. "Time to pack."

It didn't take long to throw some things for both her and Jane into a suitcase. She changed out of her uniform, choosing comfortable jeans and a navy blue cardigan sweater over a white turtleneck, but added the gun and holster.

After pulling a clean uniform from the closet, she went into Jane's room to pick out some of her daughter's favorite toys. She found the dolls easily enough, but the stuffed otter she had given the little girl during a trip to the zoo last summer was nowhere to be found.

Had Jane taken it to day care? Or had it been left in the pink backpack? Either way, she hoped her daughter didn't ask for it. Hopefully Mikey would keep her preoccupied.

Faith was just about out the door but went back for the few items of jewelry that were most precious to her. She stuffed the earrings, bracelet and pearls into her suitcase, then swept one last glance around the room.

It was distressing to realize she had no idea when she'd be back. In time for Christmas? Hopefully.

She sent up a silent prayer for God to provide strength and guidance to help her catch whoever was behind all of this.

Feeling better, she got back to work. It took a few minutes to get everything packed up in her SUV—the suitcase and Jane's toys, along with Ricci's food and water dishes, K-9 vest and toys. When they were ready, she had Ricci jump into the back, and she slid in behind the wheel.

She placed a quick call to Pete. "Hey, how are the terrible twosome?"

He laughed, causing a tingle of awareness to skate down her spine. "They've been pretty good."

She caught herself smiling at the way he'd phrased his

response. "I'm sure they've been a handful. Listen, I'm getting ready to head over, but thought I should offer to pick up something for dinner."

"I'm glad you're on the way, but no need to stop for food. I'm planning to make spaghetti and meatballs and garlic bread. Bring your appetite."

"Sounds delicious." She paused, then added, "I tried to find a hotel, but couldn't get what I needed. I'm sorry to keep bothering you, but can we stay one more night?"

"You're more than welcome to stay." His voice was low and husky. "The sofa is yours for as long as you need it."

"Thanks. You've been wonderful through all of this."

"Happy to help."

"See you shortly." She disconnected the call and decided to make a quick detour along the Jackie Robinson Parkway just to look around again. Too bad the evidence bag with Claire's blouse was still in Pete's SUV; it might have been helpful. Still, she was puzzled by the fact that Logan's car hadn't been found. Was it possible that Trevor Wilson wasn't working alone? She made a mental note to dig into Wilson's background later that evening.

Traffic wasn't its usual snarl, maybe because it was a Saturday and people had chosen to stay home after the snowstorm.

Her gaze was on the spot where Logan had been found when bright headlights came up fast behind her. She pressed hard on the accelerator, and was glancing over her shoulder to see if she could change lanes, when the car rammed into her from behind.

The collision was jarring. She tightened her grip on the steering wheel, hearing the scrabble of Ricci's nails as he was knocked off balance in the crate. Concerned for the dog's welfare, she tried to keep the SUV under control as her heart lodged in her throat.

But within seconds, the car behind her struck her again, harder this time.

The steering wheel jerked beneath her hands, and the entire vehicle shuddered from the impact. She overcorrected and felt the tires hit the curb.

The car wobbled back and forth, then careened up and over the median. As she punched the brake, bringing the SUV to an abrupt stop, the car that had hit her flew past along the parkway.

Faith tried to get a make or model of the vehicle, but all she could see was the snow-covered license plate.

SEVEN

Making dinner for Faith and the kids didn't seem like a chore. Pete wasn't sure why. Normally, he didn't think much about it, cooking was just one of those things you had to do when you were raising a child. Along with laundry, shopping, baths and bedtime stories.

The kids played well together and when they fought, they often managed to settle their differences without parental guidance. He wondered if that was a result of being in the day care together.

Which reminded him that Mikey needed a shepherd costume. The Christmas program was on Tuesday, Christmas Eve. He'd figured a white sheet cut down to Mikey's size and wrapped around him with a braided rope or twine should do the trick.

Did Faith have Jane's angel costume ready? He'd have to ask.

Twin headlights flashed through the kitchen window as a vehicle pulled into the driveway. Faith was later than he'd anticipated, and he felt his pulse kick up a notch. Reminding himself to get over it, Pete crossed to open the door and leave it ajar before returning to the spaghetti boiling on the stove.

Faith came in a few minutes later, a suitcase, laptop

case and items for Ricci bundled in her arms. The K-9 stood alert at her side. "Hi. Something smells delicious."

"Thanks." He glanced at her, picking up on her strained tone as she provided food and water for Ricci. "Should be ready in ten minutes. Are you okay?"

"It's been a rough day," she admitted. "I'll fill you in later."

"Mommy!" Jane came running into the kitchen at the sound of Faith's voice. "Where have you been?"

"Taking care of a few things." Faith lifted her daughter in her arms for a hug and a kiss. "Have you been good for Mr. Pete?"

Jane nodded vigorously. "Sometimes Mikey doesn't share very well, but he's learning."

Pete's lips twitched. He'd overheard the opposite just a few short minutes ago, but wisely held his tongue.

"I'm pretty sure you do the same thing sometimes, right?" Faith asked, as if instinctively knowing the truth.

Jane shook her head but dropped the subject. "Are we really staying over again tonight?"

"Yes, we are. I brought our things, see?" Faith gestured to the suitcase. "We'll unpack after dinner."

"Can me and Mikey sleep in the fort again?" Jane's voice rang with excitement.

"Yes, but only if you behave and share your toys nicely." Faith set Jane down.

Pete tested the noodles to make sure they were done before taking them over to the sink to be drained. "Jane, why don't you and Mikey wash your hands in the bathroom?"

"Okay!" Jane ran back to the playroom. "Mikey! The psgetti is done!"

"I'll set the table," Faith offered.

He fought the urge to pull Faith into a welcoming embrace. She looked frazzled and he wanted to reassure her, but forced himself to stay back. They weren't a couple. This forced togetherness was messing with his brain. He stayed focused on putting the garlic bread beneath the broiler while she found plates, cups and silverware.

"Get everything taken care of at the house?"

Faith grimaced and nodded. "Yeah. Nothing missing from what I can tell, which seems odd."

He had to agree. "I expected you sooner. Did something happen? You look upset."

"Yeah." She blew out a breath. "Someone rammed into me from behind on the Jackie Robinson Parkway. Brianne gave me a ride here, because my car needed to be towed."

"What?" He'd assumed she'd just taken longer at the house. "Who hit you?"

"I wish I knew." Her expression was grim. "I don't want to say anything in front of the kids."

He couldn't argue, since the kids returned from their foray to the bathroom. Mikey had missed a spot on his chin, but Pete let it go. He was troubled by Faith's collision. The danger around her was escalating and he was afraid that she'd end up hurt or worse.

Was this how his sister-in-law, Eva, felt every time Finn was in danger?

"I love psgetti," Jane announced as Faith lifted her onto her pillowed seat.

"Me, too," Mikey echoed the sentiment.

"Don't forget, we have to pray." Pete shook off his dark thoughts, setting the plate of spaghetti and meatballs, and the garlic bread, in the center of the table before taking his seat.

Faith glanced at him in surprise. "Yes, we do." She held out her hand. Pete took it, acutely aware of the warmth of her fingers within his.

He was so distracted, he missed a portion of the prayer which brought another flash of guilt.

"...and for this wonderful food You have provided for us to eat. Amen."

"Amen," he echoed.

"Amen," Jane and Mikey said at the same time. The kids looked at each other and burst into giggles.

Pete wryly shook his head as he filled Mikey's plate and then did the same for Jane. He handed the platter to Faith, who helped herself.

For several moments there was only silence as everyone began to eat.

"This is amazing, thanks, Pete." Faith's praise made the tips of his ears burn with embarrassment.

"It's nothing special." His cooking skills had been learned at the firehouse. "I'm glad the kids seem to like it."

Faith nodded, then lowered her voice. "After dinner, I'd like to tell Jane about her father."

"Understood." He met her somber gaze. "Let me know if you need anything."

Her smile was sad. "Maybe just some time alone."

"I'll give Mikey a bath." He glanced at his son, who already had spaghetti sauce in his blond hair. "He'll need it."

"Jane, too. But I think I'll talk to her first, then distract her with a bath."

"Good plan." He wished there was something more he could do to help. The conversation he'd had with Mikey seemed like eons ago, rather than just seven months. Pete realized it had been weeks since Mikey mentioned his mother or suffered any of the nightmares he had during those initial weeks after her death.

Kids were resilient; Mikey was proof of that. He knew Jane would grieve for her father but would be okay in the long run. Sad truth was that at this age, their memories faded faster than those of an adult.

The meal was a success, especially for Ricci, who had sat between the kids, benefitting from crumbs of garlic bread they dropped to the floor.

After dinner, Pete and Faith cleaned the kitchen. She insisted on washing dishes so he dried them.

"Any words of wisdom on how to tell Faith about her father's death?"

Pete let out his breath in a whoosh. "It's hard to know how much they understand at this age. Even after I explained to Mikey about his mother being up in heaven, he still asked when she was coming home, especially when I picked him up from day care. Malina did that more than I did, so Mikey was all too aware he was stuck with me."

"I'm sure it wasn't easy."

"It wasn't. But we're better now. Jane will be okay, too. I think it's harder for a young child to lose their mother than a father." It wasn't easy to admit, but he'd witnessed the impact on his son. "I know there were times Mikey wished I was the one who was up in heaven rather than his mom."

"Oh, Pete, I'm sure that's not true. Both parents are important to children."

He lifted a shoulder. "Mothers are often the primary caretakers when it comes to young kids," he countered. "And that was what made it such a difficult transition for us. Dr. Amelia Crane was very helpful."

Faith's expression turned thoughtful. "I'll call for an appointment but suspect we won't get in to see her until after Christmas."

Pete put the last of the dishes away, then hung the towel on the oven handle to dry. "Maybe not, but it could be that all the excitement of the holiday will work as a distraction."

"I hope so." She flashed him a warm smile. "Thanks again for everything you're doing for us."

"Anytime." He was surprised at how much he truly meant that. "I'll take Mikey upstairs for his bath, leaving you and Jane alone for a while."

"Thanks." Her smile faded under the weight of the conversation she needed to have with her daughter.

Pete wanted to pull her close but forced himself to take a step back. "Mikey," he called. "It's time for your bath."

"Okay."

Pete followed his son, then paused in the doorway, looking back at Faith. "You're going to do fine."

"Thanks."

Leaving Faith and Jane alone as he took Mikey upstairs for his bath wasn't easy. He wanted to be there for Faith. To support her through this difficult time.

He cared about her with a depth that frightened him.

Faith helped finish up the fort, admittedly stalling for time, before she got down to business.

"Jane, we need to talk." Faith led her daughter to the sofa that doubled as her bed. When they were settled, she looked directly into her daughter's eyes. "Honey, I have sad news about your daddy."

Jane's tiny brow furrowed with confusion. "Is he here?"

"No, I'm afraid not." Faith struggled to find the age-appropriate words to explain what had transpired. "Daddy isn't going to be around any longer. He died and went up to be with God."

"In heaven? Like an angel?"

Faith knew that her daughter had angels on the mind since she was playing the role of an angel in the Christmas program. "Kind of," she admitted. "Daddy is in heaven with his mommy and daddy. They died before you were born."

Now Jane's lower lip began to tremble. "But I don't want Daddy to be in heaven. He promised to come see my Christmas program."

"I know, honey." Faith felt tears prick her eyes and she gathered the little girl close. "Daddy loved you very much, and if he hadn't died, he would have absolutely come to your Christmas program. But God had other plans for him."

"I don't want him to watch from heaven." Faith began to cry. "I want him to be with me!"

"I know." Faith rocked Jane in her lap, wishing there was a better way to explain death to a four-year-old child.

Mikey came out from behind the sofa, freshly bathed and dressed in a pair of Spider-Man pajamas. "Jane? Your daddy is in heaven with my mommy?"

Jane sniffled and wiped her face against Faith's sweater before turning to look at Mikey. "Your mommy is in heaven, too?"

Mikey nodded. "Yep."

That seemed to get through to Jane more than anything else. She slid off Faith's lap and went over to give Mikey a hug. Watching the two kids comfort each other made tears sting her eyes once more.

Faith looked over their heads to see Pete hovering behind Mikey, his intense brown eyes full of emotion.

"Let's play in the fort," Jane said, breaking away from Mikey.

"Okay."

Deciding to forgo Jane's bath, Faith allowed the kids to go into the playroom, leaving her alone with Pete. He crossed over and dropped beside her on the sofa. She was grateful to have him there with her, offering his support.

Pete put a comforting arm around her shoulders. She basked in the warmth and his musky scent mingled with the baby shampoo he'd used on Mikey. "He'll be okay."

"Yes, because God is watching over us."

"Maybe that's true, but I was pretty mad at Him, after Malina died. And that was before I knew she'd been murdered."

"Is that why you don't go to church?" Since he'd opened the door, she decided to take it as an invitation.

"Not just that," he acknowledged. "I wasn't raised to attend church. We were taught about God as kids, but that's about it. There wasn't a lot of religion in our family."

Faith thought that was sad, yet it helped to know that Pete wasn't opposed to the idea of God and faith. "God's strength helps us through the difficult times."

He shrugged and she subtly edged a little closer. "My sister-in-law, Eva, told me the same thing. I have to admit, several months ago, I prayed while being delayed one flight after another when Mikey was kidnapped. Those were the worst hours of my life."

"Oh, Pete." Faith knew about the events from the summer, as half the K-9 team had been out searching for Mikey. "I'm sure that was horrible."

"It was worse than losing Malina," he said in a low voice. "I know that sounds harsh, but our marriage was going through a rough patch for several months before her death. She'd changed, but I was too clueless to realize that it was because of an addiction to drugs."

Her heart ached for him. "I lived through a rough patch in my marriage to Logan, too. Only his issue was another woman, not drugs. It's not easy to let go, even when you know the marriage is over."

Pete hugged her close. "We're a pair, aren't we?" His voice was little more than a whisper.

"Yes." She rested her head in the crook of his shoulder, feeling supported in a way she hadn't experienced since before Logan's affair. "A very nice pair."

He chuckled. She was glad she could make him smile. She tipped her head back to look up at him. Their gazes caught, held, and then, slowly, he lowered his mouth to hers.

His mouth was sweet yet firm, gentle yet thrilling. It had been so long since she'd been held by a man. So long since she'd been kissed.

"Mikey! Your daddy is kissing my mommy!"

Jane's words felt like a bucket of snow had been dumped over their heads. Pete lifted his head with a low groan.

"We're not going to hear the end of this," he whispered.

"Nope." She smiled because she really didn't care.

She'd treasure this kiss for a long time to come.

EIGHT

Pete couldn't believe how right it had felt to kiss Faith. How perfectly she'd fit into his arms. But he wished the kids hadn't witnessed their embrace because they quickly peppered them with questions.

"Do you love my mommy?" Jane asked.

"Are Jane and her mommy going to live with us forever?" Mikey wanted to know.

He and Faith did their best to distract the kids with making their costumes for the upcoming Christmas program at the day care. One bedsheet cut in half worked perfectly for one angel dress and one shepherd robe. Finally the kids fell asleep in their fort.

"Whew," Faith said, collapsing on the sofa. "That wasn't easy."

"Nope. But hey, at least we have a head start on the costumes." Pete remained standing and gestured to the stairs. "Give me a minute to head up to grab a blanket and pillow for you."

"Thanks." Her warm smile was enough to tempt him into kissing her again. "Oh, and I'd like to attend church in the morning." She paused, then added, "No pressure. You and Mikey don't have to join us."

His first instinct was to refuse, but instead he found himself nodding. "Okay, that works. What time?"

"Service starts at ten and the church isn't far from the K-9 Command Unit."

He nodded. "Sounds good." After providing Faith a blanket and pillow, he stood awkwardly for a moment. "Well, uh, good night."

"Good night, Peter."

It was the first time she'd used his full name and it caught him off guard. No one ever used his full name, even Malina hadn't, but he liked the way Faith said it.

Truthfully, there were many things he liked about Faith. But remembering how much he'd once loved Malina, only to have things end so badly, caused him to back off. He returned to his room upstairs, telling himself Faith was only there because she and Jane needed to be safe, nothing more.

The following morning, he woke up to the enticing scent of bacon and eggs. Filled with a sense of anticipation, and with his stomach growling, he quickly showered and dressed before heading down to the kitchen.

Thankfully, the topic of discussion was the shepherd and angel costumes, and not their ill-timed kiss.

"Good morning." Faith's smile warmed his heart. "I was thinking we could stop at the craft store after church to pick up the items we need to finish the costumes."

"Not a problem." He helped himself to coffee. "You didn't have to cook."

"It's my turn—you made dinner last night." She'd scrambled the eggs and was finishing up the bacon. "It's almost ready."

He took a seat at the table, reminding himself how this situation was temporary. He couldn't afford to get too accustomed to having Faith and Jane around.

No matter how nice it was.

Faith set everything on the table, then led them in prayer. After making sure both kids had their food, he eagerly dug into his breakfast.

"This is great," he praised her. Faith's blush made him grin. Then he turned serious. "Have you heard anything more from Zimmerman?"

"Not yet." Her brow furrowed. "I sure hope they find Trevor, and soon."

"Me, too." He found it difficult to understand why the guy was out on bail in the first place.

The meal went by quickly. Deep down, Pete admitted he wasn't looking forward to attending church. He wasn't exactly sure what to expect but took a moment to stress with Mikey how important it was for him to behave.

After cleaning up the kitchen, and taking Ricci outside for a quick bathroom break, they piled into the SUV. Faith had decided to bring Ricci along for protection, especially as they'd promised the kids they'd stop at the craft store after church to get a belt for Mikey's robe and wings for Jane's angel.

Pete noticed that Faith kept a keen eye on the cars behind them via her passenger-side window. After the events of the day before, he couldn't blame her for being suspicious of everyone and everything. Especially since her call to Detective Zimmerman had gone unanswered.

When they entered the modest yet pretty white church, he was surprised to see several familiar faces. Eva and Finn were talking to another couple. His sister-in-law didn't see him at first; she suffered from retinitis pigmentosa, a condition that slowly caused blindness. He knew her peripheral vision was compromised, the same way Malina's had been. But then she turned, her eyes lighting up with pleasure as she quickly came over.

"I'm so happy to see you." She gave Pete a quick hug, and then did the same with Faith, before crouching down in front of Mikey. "How are you, Mikey?"

Pete felt guilty for not bringing Mikey to church services before now. It was clear from the way Eva and Faith were greeted by the other church members that this was more than a simple service. It was a close-knit community. A place where a single dad would never feel lonely.

As the service progressed, Pete wasn't bored. The pastor told stories even the children could relate to. Mikey and Jane behaved better than he'd anticipated. The theme centering on the importance of forgiveness made him realize how he needed to let go of his grudge against Malina.

When the service was over, Pete felt an overwhelming sense of peace. Faith took the kids and Ricci outside, but he lingered for a moment, staring at the altar, wondering why he'd resisted attending for so long.

Outside, dark storm clouds hovered overhead. He noticed Faith and the kids were waiting inside his SUV as cars were streaming out of the parking lot.

He felt someone come up behind him. As he turned to look, something hard came down on the back of his head. Pain reverberated through his skull, then all went dark.

Faith twisted in her seat to look out the rear window, wondering what was taking Pete so long. Her eyes widened in horror as she noticed a crumpled form lying on the slushy ground. Recognizing Pete's jacket caused her heart to squeeze painfully in her chest.

"Pete!" She raked her gaze over the area, searching for an assailant, but didn't find anyone suspicious. Still, she hesitated to leave the kids alone in the car. She leaned over and opened the back hatch, letting Ricci out. Then she slid out from the passenger seat, making sure the doors were locked before she followed her K-9 partner.

Ricci growled low in his throat as he sniffed the ground around Pete. Had her partner recognized the scent as being the same one left behind by the intruder in her home?

"Pete!" She rushed over to crouch beside him. "Are you okay?"

He let out a low groan and lifted his head, glancing around in confusion. "Faith? What happened? Who hit me?"

"You tell me." She searched his eyes, grateful to note his pupils were equal. "Can you stand?"

"Yeah." She helped him to his feet as Ricci continued to growl low in his throat, sniffing the area.

"Ricci picked up your attacker's scent." She didn't like being out in the open like this. "Let's get you into the SUV."

Faith helped him get into the passenger seat, then turned to Ricci. "Find!"

Her K-9 sniffed the ground and the air, then headed off to the farthest corner of the parking lot. He stopped and sat, continuing to growl low in his throat.

She stood for a moment, trying to understand where the assailant had gone. Into a car? She looked back at the line of cars disappearing out of the parking lot.

Remembering the vehicle that had hit her from behind, she wondered if any of the cars waiting had front end damage.

"Come, Ricci." She took off toward the line of vehicles, looking carefully at each car and then at the driver.

None had damage, and no one behind the wheel looked like either Trevor Wilson or Claire Munch.

Her shoulders slumped with defeat. Whoever attacked

Pete was long gone. And worse? The perp had gone from targeting her, to hurting Pete.

Faith decided she and Jane would stay Sunday night, mostly because she was worried about Pete's head injury. Not to mention the small detail of not having a vehicle of her own to drive.

Pete claimed he was fine, and that he didn't even have much of a headache, but he'd agreed to relax for the day. She tried to talk him out of going to work the following morning, but he insisted he couldn't call off this close to the holiday.

Monday morning was chaotic, but they eventually hit the road, dropping the kids off at day care first. Faith asked Peggy to stay alert for any danger, and she agreed.

"I'll get a new police vehicle today, so after work I can pick up Jane and we'll head back to our place." She darted him a quick glance. "I'm sure you're sick of having houseguests."

Pete frowned. "Are you sure it's safe?"

"Better for you and Mikey if I stay far away."

"I told you, I'm fine." His voice had a bit of an edge, as if he were embarrassed that he'd been attacked.

But she knew that his injury was her fault and no one else's. The guilt was difficult to ignore.

"Listen, if you want to head back to your place, that's fine." Pete glanced at her, his dark eyes serious. "But Jane should probably stay with us for the next couple of days."

She couldn't deny there was some logic to Pete's suggestion. So far, none of the attacks had been near his home. Except she had seen the suspicious car with the snow-covered license plate drive past that first night.

A shiver lifted the hairs along the back of her neck. The thought of Pete being there alone with the kids was worrisome. "I'll think about it," she reluctantly agreed, "and call you later, okay?"

Pete nodded, and their gazes locked and held for a long moment. There was so much she wanted to say but she couldn't find the words. She smiled, then forced herself to get out of the car and head inside the NYC K-9 Command Unit.

As she and Ricci entered the building, her cell phone rang. Recognizing Zimmerman's number, she quickly answered. "Officer Johnson."

"Detective Zimmerman, returning your call."

She swallowed a flash of temper. "Thanks for calling back, Detective. I'd like to know if you have any new information to share about my ex-husband's murder."

There was a pause before he responded. "Nothing new, I'm afraid. We're still trying to locate Claire Munch and Trevor Wilson. We've heard through some of Wilson's known associates that he has a meeting with his lawyer early this afternoon. We're hoping to pick him up for questioning there."

She was encouraged by that news. "That's great. I'd like to be there."

"It's not necessary—we can handle it."

His dismissive tone put her on edge. "What about forensic evidence?"

There was another long pause, giving her the impression he was trying to figure out how much to tell her.

"I'm a cop," she pointed out. "Has the autopsy been done?"

"It was finished first thing this morning," he reluctantly admitted. "Not much information to be gleaned, though. The ME believes our victim was stabbed with a hunting knife."

The image was all too real, but she kept her voice steady. "Any idea if the perp was male or female?"

"The ME wouldn't provide a judgment call on that. Said that it could be either."

She tried to think of something else to ask, but nothing came to mind. "I'd be interested to know if the crime scene techs were able to get any trace evidence from my house."

"That's going to take a while." Zimmerman's tone wasn't encouraging. "Why don't you relax and focus on taking care of yourself and your daughter? Christmas is in two days, I'm sure we'll know more after the holiday."

The way he treated her like a civilian instead of a cop grated on her nerves. But there was nothing to be gained by arguing with him. "Please keep me informed of your progress."

She disconnected without giving him a chance to respond. Jerk. Threading her way through the cubicles of the NYC K-9 Command Unit office, she sought out Brianne. "Hey, any news?"

"Not yet, but I'm meeting Zimmerman outside Trevor Wilson's lawyer's office this afternoon. If he shows for his appointment, we're going to grab him."

"I heard and I'd like to tag along. And before you say no, understand that Pete was attacked outside church yesterday and Ricci picked up the perp's scent. I believe it's the same person who ransacked my place. If Trevor Wilson is guilty, Ricci might let us know."

"Okay," Brianne agreed. "I'll clear it with Chief Jameson."

"Thanks." Faith was glad she'd be included. "Zimmerman told me the only thing he learned from the autopsy was that the weapon was likely a hunting knife."

Brianne nodded. "Makes me think Trevor Wilson is our guy. He likes to hunt and fish upstate, a real outdoorsman."

Just like Logan, which was interesting. Faith thought that Brianne was right. Would Wilson actually show for his lawyer appointment? Hopefully he wouldn't take off, disappear somewhere they'd never find him. "Well, there has to be some other angle to investigate. Have all of Wilson's known associates been checked out?"

"I have two more names to check, but the others all claimed they haven't seen him." Brianne shrugged and glanced down at her K-9, Stella. "As long as we don't get a bomb threat, I should be able to check them out before meeting Zimmerman."

"Let me know when you and Stella are ready to roll."

"Will do," Brianne promised.

Faith used the morning to dig further into Claire Munch's background, since she hadn't been assigned any new cases. There had to be someone who knew where her ex-husband's fiancée was staying.

Given the upcoming holiday, and Faith's own recent experience, it didn't seem likely Claire had sought refuge in a hotel. No, the more she thought about it, the more she suspected the woman was hiding out somewhere. With a friend or colleague.

Colleague! Faith racked her brain for a moment, trying to remember. Hadn't Logan mentioned Claire worked as a receptionist in a doctor's office? An OB/GYN physician group if she remembered correctly.

She immediately began searching the OB/GYN offices nearby, calling them one by one, asking for Claire Munch. She was on her third call, waiting on hold, when her cell phone rang. Hanging up on the OB's office, she answered the call.

"Johnson."

"Faith? It's Brianne. Are you ready to go?"

"Yes. We'll meet you out front." Faith picked up Ricci's

leash and hurried downstairs to meet Brianne. Since she didn't have her assigned vehicle yet, she put Ricci in the back seat and slid in next to Brianne.

The law office wasn't far. When Brianne pulled up, she peered through the windshield. "I hope he shows," Faith said.

"He will." Brianne sounded confident. "Let's go."

Faith and Ricci followed Brianne and Stella as they crossed over to join Zimmerman and another detective, Bob Durran. Zimmerman frowned when he saw Faith and Ricci but didn't say anything.

"I need you and Officer Johnson to stay back and watch the perimeter, in case he makes a break for it," Zimmerman said. "He's inside now—we're going to grab him when he leaves."

Faith knew he was trying to minimize their involvement and glanced at Brianne, who reluctantly nodded.

The detectives took up positions on either side of the door leading into the building. Faith was stationed across the street down a few yards from Zimmerman, as Brianne and Stella took up a position, also across the street but farther down from Detective Durran.

Ten minutes went by before Faith recognized the bulky man who'd once kidnapped his own son emerging from the building. The two detectives moved in, but Wilson took off across the street, darting between cars.

"Get him!" Faith commanded quickly, taking Ricci off leash.

Ricci tore after Wilson, easily catching up with him, barking like crazy. Wilson let out a frightened shriek.

"Get him off me! Get him off!"

"Watch him," Faith commanded as she closed the gap.

Ricci stood in front of Wilson, continuing to bark as a way of warning the perp he'd better not try to run.

Zimmerman and Durran moved faster than she'd expected them to in order to catch up with them.

"Ricci, heel," Faith commanded.

The two detectives frisked Wilson, finding a gun in his jacket pocket.

"Well, look at this." Zimmerman held the gun up for Faith to see. "Trevor Wilson, you are under arrest for illegally carrying a firearm along with a potential charge of murder."

"I'm not saying anything without my lawyer," Wilson whined. "And keep that woman and her dog away from me."

Faith rested her hand on Ricci's head as Zimmerman and Durran hauled Wilson to their vehicle. Brianne joined her.

"We've got him, Faith. He has a gun and with a search order we might even find the hunting knife. Hopefully his lawyer will convince him to cooperate."

"Yeah." Faith nodded. "I guess this means the danger is over."

"Merry Christmas." Brianne gave her a quick hug. "Let's head back to the Command Unit."

Faith's sense of overwhelming relief was quickly followed by a wave of depression. There was no longer a good reason to stay with Pete Stallings.

It was time for them to go their separate ways.

NINE

When Faith arrived at his place after her shift, Pete was happy to hear Trevor Wilson had been taken into custody but was bummed when Faith quickly packed their things, declaring it was time for them to head home.

"Staying one more night wouldn't hurt," he pointed out in a pathetic attempt to convince her to remain.

"You've been more than gracious, Peter, but with Wilson in jail, we'll be fine." Her gaze clung to his for a long, poignant moment. "Besides, I'll see you tomorrow at the Christmas program, right?"

"Right. Three o'clock. Don't forget Jane's angel costume." He'd stopped at the craft store on his lunch break to get what they needed, since they hadn't gone after church. He'd also gotten permission to leave work early to attend the program. As it was Christmas Eve, the day care closed an hour earlier, at four in the afternoon instead of five. "Wouldn't miss it."

"Me, either." Faith crossed the room to give him a quick hug. "Thanks again."

He held her close, breathing in her familiar vanilla-and-cranberry scent, reluctant to let her go. "My pleasure," he whispered.

When she stepped back, he wanted nothing more than to stop her from leaving, but of course, he didn't.

"Jane, are you ready to go?" Faith called.

"No! Don't wanna go! Wanna stay with Mikey!" Jane's voice came from the playroom.

"Yeah, me, too!" Mikey agreed.

Pete couldn't help but smile. "Best friends."

"Until the next fight." Faith left her suitcase in the kitchen to get her daughter. Pete followed, his grin widening when he saw the kids were standing side by side, holding hands. "Jane, say goodbye to Mikey. It's time to go home."

Jane lifted her hand clasped tightly with Mikey's. "We can't. We glued our hands together."

"You…what?" Faith asked. "What kind of glue?"

"White glue," Mikey explained helpfully. He looked at Jane and giggled. "We're stuck together forever."

"Yeah. Forever." Jane bobbed her head in agreement.

Faith threw him a frustrated look and he shrugged. It wasn't his idea. "Hey, at least it's not superglue."

"That's not funny." Her initial anger quickly faded as she sighed. "I just hope it comes out with soap and water."

"It will." At least, he thought it would.

The task of separating the kids glued hands took longer than he'd anticipated. When they finished, the kids hugged each other as if they were being separated for the rest of their lives, rather than twelve hours.

Faith looked frazzled by the time she left with Ricci and Jane.

And his house seemed unbearably empty without them.

He did his best to keep up the normal pattern of bath time and a story before bed for Mikey's sake.

Long after Mikey was asleep, Pete sat on the sofa, wondering how a woman and her daughter could have changed his life so dramatically in such a short time.

And then an idea popped into his mind. He smiled, as he understood exactly what he could give Faith for Christmas.

Faith couldn't believe how strange it felt to be in her own home. It didn't make sense—she'd only spent a couple nights at Pete's.

Her home should feel like a home. Not silent and empty.

She put the finishing touches on Jane's angel costume, then walked from window to window with Ricci at her side. Everything was quiet outside and Trevor Wilson was in custody.

Still, she didn't sleep well, waking every couple of hours at the slightest sound.

In the morning, she drove Jane to the day-care center, hoping to catch a glimpse of Pete and Mikey. But apparently she'd just missed Pete, as Mikey came running over to greet Jane like a long-lost friend.

Faith stood for a moment, watching Jane's dark head next to Mikey's blond one, before turning to leave. She couldn't help feeling depressed that she'd missed Pete. Which was crazy since she'd see him in a few hours.

At the NYC K-9 Command Unit, things were busy. Phones were ringing and there was a lot of chatter about several suspicious packages that had been left near subway stations.

Obviously, Brianne and Stella would be busy with this new threat, so there was no point in asking for an update on the Trevor Wilson case.

Remembering the calls she'd made to the various OB/GYN offices in the area to try to find where Logan's fiancée, Claire, had worked, she reviewed her notes and picked up her phone to try again.

"This is Dr. Nelson's office. How may I help you?"

"This is Officer Johnson and I'm looking for Claire Munch. I believe she works for Dr. Nelson." Faith chose her words carefully, knowing that no one wanted to give out personal information about their employees.

"No, she does not," the woman replied swiftly. "He let her go weeks ago."

Let her go? "But she did work there, correct?"

"Yes. What is your name? Maybe I need to verify who I'm speaking with."

"I'm Police Officer Faith Johnson, working in the NYC K-9 Command Unit. Would you like my badge number? I'm happy to transfer you over to my boss if needed."

That seemed to mollify the woman. "Okay, yes. Claire Munch worked here. But as I said, she was let go a few weeks ago."

"Why?"

There was a long pause before the woman finally admitted, "I honestly don't know. Dr. Nelson didn't go into detail. He just told me that if anyone called for a reference I was supposed to only give her dates of service and nothing more."

That seemed odd. "Okay. I'd like to speak to Dr. Nelson, please."

"He's not here, he's at Mercy Medical Center delivering a baby."

Of course he was. "Will you please give him my name and number and have him call me as soon as possible?"

"Sure."

Faith provided her contact information, then disconnected from the call. Pensively, she glanced down at Ricci stretched out at her feet. "So, partner, why was Claire let go?"

Ricci didn't answer.

"I still think it's possible she's involved in something illegal. Even if Trevor Wilson was the one who stabbed Logan, there's something fishy with her. It seems obvious she's in danger. Why else would she be in hiding?"

Ricci thumped his tail on the floor.

"Hmm." She drummed her fingers on the table, trying to come up with her next move. No way was she going to sit around and wait for Zimmerman to come up with something. "Maybe we should talk to Wilson for ourselves."

Ricci thumped his tail again, then stretched and stood beside her as if understanding they were ready to go. She made a quick call to the jail, only to hear that Wilson was meeting with his lawyer and wasn't giving interviews yet.

She spent the rest of the day trying to get information on the forensic evidence from her place. It took several hours, but Danielle, their tech guru, was finally able to confirm that they'd gotten a partial fingerprint from her house, but so far hadn't found a match in the database.

Odd, since they had Wilson's fingerprints on file.

Troubled by that bit of news, Faith headed to the day-care center. Traffic was horrible, but thankfully she arrived five minutes before the Christmas program was about to start.

Moving through the crowd of parents and relatives, she searched for Pete.

"Faith!"

She turned and saw him waving her over, a broad smile on his face. Her heart thumped in her chest and she knew she was in trouble.

Big, big trouble.

She shouldn't be so happy to see him, when they hadn't even been apart a full twenty-four hours. But that knowledge didn't prevent her from quickly making her way over to his side.

"Hey, how are you?" She winced at her inane attempt at conversation.

"Good, you?"

"Great." She glanced around the crowded day care. "Wow, this place is packed."

"Yeah." Pete hesitated, then asked, "I was wondering if you and Jane had plans for Christmas?"

His question caught her off guard. "I—um—nothing other than spending a quiet night at home. Why?"

"I just thought it might be nice to have dinner together. The kids would love it."

Just the kids? She tried to read his expression, but then Peggy Harris loudly clapped her hands to get everyone's attention.

"Thanks for coming. The children have been working hard these past few days and we'd like to present our version of the birth of Jesus."

Faith focused her attention on the kids who were gathered at the front of the room. The kids playing Mary and Joseph were easy to spot, as were the three Wise Men. She noticed there was a baby doll in the manger and remembered how the year before they'd tried to use a real baby, but that hadn't gone well as the infant screamed through the entire program.

The memory made her smile. Mary and Joseph were flanked by a group of shepherds on one side, and a group of angels on the other.

It was easy to pick out Mikey and Jane. She waved at her daughter positioned off to the side with the rest of the angels, who waved back.

The show started with Mary and Joseph claiming there wasn't room for them at the inn, but that they were thankful to be out in the stable with a roof over their heads.

Suddenly, Mikey shouted, "Jane! Jane!"

What in the world? She glanced back at the group of angels, but this time, there was no sign of her daughter.

"Stranger Danger! Jane's gone!" Mikey continued to shout.

The interruption caused chaos, as parents looked at each other in confusion. Faith and Ricci immediately wove through the crowd to get up to the front of the room near where a group of day-care workers were standing.

"Mikey, where is Jane? Did she go to the bathroom?" The facilities were located behind where the program was being performed.

"No! The lady took her."

What lady? Faith raked her gaze over the group of day-care workers. "Did anyone see Jane? Or a woman taking Jane?"

"I thought she was with the other angels," Peggy said.

"She was, but she's not now." Panic tightened her throat and she quickly knelt in front of Mikey. "What did the lady look like?"

"A lady," Mikey repeated. He turned and pointed to a back doorway. "They went that way." His lower lip began to tremble. "I don't think Jane wanted to go with her but she had a stuffed animal that Jane wanted. She should have yelled Stranger Danger."

A vice of fear tightened around Faith's chest. She reached over and grabbed Peggy's hand. "I need Jane's coat." When the woman looked at her blankly, she gave her arm a shake. "Jane's coat! Hurry!"

"What can I do?" Pete asked.

"Nothing, yet. I have to find Jane."

"I'll come with you."

Faith appreciated Pete's support, but still wanted to rant and rave and scream at the top of her lungs. She couldn't believe Jane was missing. And who had taken her? Which woman? Someone working for Trevor Wilson? Did he have someone doing his dirty work? Like a sister? Or maybe a new girlfriend?

But if that was the case, why hadn't Jane yelled out in fear?

Or could it be Claire? A shiver rippled down her spine. Jane knew Claire. But why would Logan's fiancée take Jane? Nothing made any sense.

The seconds went by in slow motion, but finally Peggy handed her Jane's coat.

She put Jane's coat under Ricci's nose. "Find, Ricci. Find Jane."

Ricci immediately went to work, sniffing around the floor of the day-care center. He alerted on the spot where Jane had been standing with the other angels, then headed toward the back door.

Faith trusted Ricci and continued praising her partner as they went outside. The back door led to an alley, and she wondered if there had been a car waiting for the woman who'd taken her daughter.

"Find Jane," she repeated.

Ricci turned in a circle, then sat on the same spot, looking up at her with imploring eyes. It was clear he wanted to find Jane as much as she did.

"What now?" Pete asked.

She shook her head, feeling completely helpless. "I'm not sure. If there was a car waiting…" Her voice trailed off. She didn't even want to think about where the vehicle could be by now.

"Mikey said a lady took her. Who would want Jane?"

"A friend of Trevor Wilson's or maybe Claire." Faith suddenly snapped her fingers. "You still have the evidence bag containing Claire's blouse in your car, right? Please grab it."

Pete vanished back into the day-care center. She took Ricci out of the alley and looked up and down the street.

Which way had they gone? There was a subway stop several blocks in one direction, and a plethora of stores to use as hiding spots in the other.

Pulling out her phone, she quickly called in to the NYC K-9 Command Unit, requesting video surveillance of the subway station and intersections nearby as well as Brianne and Stella to assist in a search. If whoever had taken Jane was on foot, they stood a good chance of finding them.

Pete returned not only with Claire's blouse, but their winter coats. After hastily pulling on her coat, she offered the blouse scent to Ricci. Her K-9 partner sniffed Claire's scent for long moments, then went to work.

He alerted at the back door of the day-care center, and again out on the street. Both gave Faith a thin thread of hope.

If Claire had been there, she must be the one who'd taken Jane.

Now she and Pete just had to find them.

TEN

Walking alongside Faith and Ricci, Pete relived those moments six months ago when Mikey had been kidnapped. Eva and Finn had found him, basically safe and unharmed, but Pete knew things could have ended very differently.

He prayed for Jane, that she'd be safe from harm, and that Faith and Ricci would find her very soon. The little girl had wiggled her way into his heart, and Pete knew that he would do anything to help Faith find Jane and bring her home.

He couldn't imagine life without Faith and Jane.

They were a package deal and he wanted to have them both in his life for a long time.

Forever.

He caught a glimpse of a sparkly angel wing. Jane? He grasped Faith's arm. "Over there. On the sidewalk leading toward the subway."

"Hey, Claire! Stop! Police! Get her, Ricci!"

Pete caught a glimpse of a woman with blond hair carrying a little girl with dark hair wearing angel wings. A pink backpack was slung over the woman's shoulder and he recognized it as the one Faith had pulled from her police vehicle the night Logan was stabbed. Claire had almost reached the subway entrance and the staircase leading down into the station.

Ricci darted after them, quickly catching up to Claire. With a low growl, he grabbed on to the back of Claire's coat with his teeth, tugging hard in an effort to hold her back. Bystanders glanced around in confusion, thinking the K-9 was hurting Claire, rather than understanding that the little girl who didn't even have a winter coat on was the one in danger.

"Mommy!" Jane cried, pushing against Claire as a stuffed animal fell to the ground. *"Mommy!"*

The little girl's scream ripped at his heart. Faith sprinted toward them, and Pete followed. Claire looked back at them, then pulled a small gun out of her pocket and pointed it at them. "Stop right there or I'll shoot!"

Pete froze, unwilling to do anything that would cause Jane harm.

"You don't want to do this, Claire," Faith said, coming to an abrupt halt.

Ricci stood firmly in front of Claire and Jane, letting out staccato barks. Claire pointed her gun in jerky movements from Ricci to Faith and back to Ricci.

"Get back!" Claire shrieked. "Make him stop barking!"

The gun had everyone backing off, leaving a wide-open area between Faith, Ricci and Claire.

"Stay, Ricci," Faith said in a firm tone.

Ricci stopped barking and stood there, his body quivering with the desire to go after Claire.

"Don't do this, Claire," Faith repeated. Her tone was reasonable, but Pete noticed that she was inching toward Claire.

"Jane is mine! I deserve to have her!" Claire was sounding more hysterical by the moment.

Faith inched closer. Claire's gun hand lowered a bit as

if she was getting tired from holding on to Jane, the back-pack and the gun.

Pete found himself holding his breath, hoping, praying this would end well.

The gun dropped a little lower. Faith abruptly shouted, "Jump!"

Ricci leaped up onto Claire, knocking her off balance. Faith rushed forward, grabbing the gun and wrenching it out of Claire's hand.

"Noooo," Claire wailed as Faith tugged Jane out of her grasp. "You can have another baby! I can't! Give me Jane. I need Jane!"

"I'll take her." Pete shrugged out of his coat so he could wrap it around the shivering girl. As a paramedic, he was concerned about possible hypothermia. Jane was too young to be outside in the cold without a coat. Especially with the windchill in the subzero range.

Faith hesitated just a fraction of a second before relinquishing her daughter. Then she took out her handcuffs and quickly clasped one of the metal bracelets around Claire's wrist.

"You're under arrest for attempted kidnapping," Faith said as she tried to grab Claire's other flailing hand.

"No!" With superhuman strength, Claire wrenched out of Faith's grasp. She tried to run, but Ricci didn't let her get far. He lunged at her, barking furiously. When she tried to move, he locked his jaw around her ankle and hung on with all his might. Claire was no match for the ninety-pound K-9 cop. "Let me go!"

Faith took Claire down to the pavement, finally getting both cuffs secured around her wrists.

Pete had Jane huddled within his coat, watching as Faith dragged Claire to her feet. Ignoring the chill, he focused on Jane. The little girl's face was pale, her lips tinged blue from the cold. He took comfort in the fact that she was still shivering, which was a good sign. It was when the shivering stopped that you really had to worry.

He tugged the edges of the coat closer around her. "Are you warming up?" he asked.

Jane nodded.

"Jane, why did you go with Claire?" Pete asked.

"She said...I had to go with her to get my otter. She said Daddy would want me to. Then she said I belonged to her now—because my mommy didn't want me anymore." Jane's voice was soft, her teeth chattering.

"That's not true, Jane," Pete said. "Your mommy loves you very much. Claire lied to you, but you're safe now."

A cop car pulled up beside them, and Detective Zimmerman got out from behind the wheel. "I see you found Claire Munch."

"No thanks to you," Pete muttered under his breath.

"She took Jane from the day-care center in an attempt to kidnap her." Faith pushed the woman in cuffs toward Zimmerman. "She's been babbling about how she can't have kids so she needs Jane."

Zimmerman nodded. "Yeah, when I finally tracked her to the OB/GYN office where she used to work, I found out that she was fired because she tried to steal a baby. The doc didn't want to press charges, claimed he didn't want his reputation to be dragged down into the mud, so there's no record of the attempt on file."

Pete looked up at Zimmerman, unable to hide his anger. "If you knew that much, why didn't you tell Faith? She had a right to know her daughter was in danger."

"I just found out this morning," Zimmerman protested. "One of the neighbors mentioned the argument between her and Logan was something about fighting for custody. How was I to know she wanted to steal a kid?"

"Even knowing that would have helped." Pete's tone was tight with anger. It was tempting to flatten the guy where he stood but Pete knew that assaulting a police officer wasn't smart.

"Why did you do it, Claire?" Faith asked. "Why did you kill Logan?"

"I didn't mean to, but he was going to break up with me. He said I was crazy. But I'm not crazy—I just want a baby. A child. Jane." Claire looked beseechingly at Faith. "You understand, don't you?"

"No, I don't." Faith's tone was clipped. She patted the woman's pockets and pulled out a small disposable phone.

"I didn't mean to kill him." Claire began to sob. "The knife was in the glove box. He told me I was crazy. And that it was over. I followed him out of the car. I didn't mean to kill him!"

Pete looked at Faith, who appeared stunned by the news. The person behind all of this wasn't Trevor Wilson, after all, but Claire. Pete longed to hug Faith close but needed to keep Jane warm. He was still concerned about the little girl being exposed for too long in the cold winter air.

It was horrible to realize that Logan had been killed with his own hunting knife.

The danger was over, but Pete didn't want this to be the end of his time with Faith and Jane.

He wanted, needed, for this to be just the beginning.

Faith couldn't believe that Claire Munch was the one who'd killed Logan and had tried multiple times to kill her.

All because Claire wanted to have Jane for herself. Which made no sense, since killing Faith wouldn't mean she'd get custody of Jane.

And she'd been wrong about Trevor. He hadn't hurt Logan, despite having an illegal weapon. She shivered as they returned to the day-care center. She carried Jane in Pete's coat, thankful for his thoughtfulness. When they returned, they found that some of the parents had left to help search, others had taken their kids and gone home. Peggy Harris and the other teachers were relieved to see Jane had been rescued and apologized for how it had happened.

"She said she was one of the kid's aunts, and even though I didn't recognize her, we have several kids who only come part-time, so I didn't think too much about it," Peggy confessed. "I'm so sorry. I didn't see her up front. I'm not sure how she got close enough to grab Jane."

Faith didn't like it but could understand how difficult it might be to recognize every adult during an event like this. "It's okay, but maybe next year we should make the parents and relatives meet up with their respective kids so this can't happen."

Peggy blew out a breath. "Maybe there shouldn't be a next time. I thought the Christmas program was a good idea, but wow, this one was a horrible disaster."

Faith shook her head. "You can't think about it like that. Christmas is a special time of the year. I know how much both Mikey and Jane looked forward to participating in the program."

"I guess." Peggy didn't look entirely convinced.

"Faith is right," Pete spoke up. "Don't let one bad experience keep you from celebrating the birth of Jesus."

Faith was touched by his response and turned to kneel beside Mikey. "Thanks for telling us when Jane went missing. If you hadn't spoken up, we may not have found her so quickly."

"I love Jane," Mikey said. "And I hate that lady."

Faith smiled. "I know, but God teaches us that we need to forgive others, so you shouldn't hate her. Especially since she's sick and needs help." A lot of help, she thought to herself. The crazed look in Claire's eyes would stay with her for a long time.

Faith didn't think Claire Munch was entirely sane or rational, but that was something for the courts to address. As long as she and Jane were safe, that was all that mattered.

"Ready to head home?" Pete asked.

She rose to her feet and nodded. "Yes."

He hesitated, then asked, "My home or yours? I don't think you and Jane should be alone right now. Especially on Christmas Eve."

Since she didn't really want to be alone, she nodded. "Yours. My tree is still a disaster."

Pete's smile stole her breath. She realized, then and there, how wonderful it had been to have his support during those long moments when Claire had Jane.

She cared about him and Mikey and didn't want to stop seeing them.

Yet she knew it might be too soon for Pete. His wife had only died seven months ago. He'd drawn that amazing family portrait for Mikey out of love.

As she bundled Jane into her coat, Faith told herself there was no rush. That maybe, over time, Pete might come to care for her and Jane.

They each drove their own vehicle to Pete's house. As she walked inside, Faith was startled by the feeling of coming home.

"I—uh, pulled out steaks for dinner." Pete looked embarrassed. "I was hoping to convince you and Jane to come over after the play even before all this happened."

She burst out laughing. "Guess your devious plan worked, huh?"

He chuckled and spread his hands. "I also have chicken tenders for the kids. Not sure about Jane, but Mikey doesn't love steak medium rare."

"Chicken tenders!" Mikey jumped up and down. "Yummy in my tummy!"

Jane nodded but was more subdued. Faith's heart ached for her daughter, knowing how frightening it must have been to be taken by Claire.

"Would you both like to watch a movie?" Pete asked. "I think I can find *How the Grinch Stole Christmas.* Dinner will be ready by the time it's over."

"Jane?" Mikey turned to his best friend. "Will you watch Grinch with me?"

"Okay." Jane smiled at Mikey. "But I want Ricci to sit with us."

Faith understood her daughter still didn't feel safe and was glad Ricci would be there for her.

"Maybe you should wrap up in a blanket," Pete suggested as the kids crawled up onto the love seat facing the TV. "And Ricci can sit right beside you, too."

Faith was amazed at how Pete jumped in to help care for Jane. He was a wonderful father. She glanced at the framed family drawings on the wall and reminded herself that Pete's loss hadn't been very long ago.

Dinner was delicious. Pete had not only made amazing steaks, but grilled asparagus and red potatoes. Logan had never bothered to cook a meal for her, and while she knew it wasn't fair, she couldn't help comparing the differences between the two men.

Pete was gentle, kind and caring. He didn't need to prove himself to be macho. And he took fatherhood seriously, putting Mikey's needs first.

The same way she did with Jane. She admired so much about him. The way he'd stayed by her side while she and Ricci tracked Claire, the way he'd taken Jane and helped warm her up.

The way he'd kissed Faith as if he'd never let her go.

When the dishes were done, she took Ricci outside. She was glad Claire Munch was behind bars, where she belonged. She knew Trevor Wilson would do some time for illegally carrying a gun, but she wasn't worried about him. She thought for sure that Wilson would stay far, far away.

When she entered Pete's house, she found him and the kids in the living room. She was stunned to find three presents beneath the Christmas tree, one especially large one and two smaller ones.

"What's this?" she asked, crossing over to sit beside Pete on the sofa. She was embarrassed that she didn't have anything to give him in exchange.

"Well, it's not much but I thought it would be nice to open a couple of presents tonight." He put his arm around her shoulders and brought her in for a brief hug.

"But I don't have anything for you."

Pete's smile widened. "Just having you here with me tonight is the only gift I need. We'll let the kids each open theirs first, okay?"

Her throat was so thick with emotion, she could barely speak. "Okay."

"Here, Jane." Mikey handed her one gift. "This one is for you."

"How do you know?" Jane asked.

"My name starts with M. That's a J." Mikey grabbed his gift and sat beside her. "Let's open them at the same time."

"Okay." They looked at each other, giggled, then ripped open their gifts in record time.

"Legos!" they cried in unison.

Faith inwardly groaned and elbowed Pete in the ribs. "What were you thinking? We'll be stepping on bits of plastic for weeks."

"Hey, it will keep them occupied for hours," Pete argued.

"Can we play with our gifts now?" Mikey asked.

"Sure, go ahead. Oh, wait, Mikey, bring Faith's present over for her."

"It's big," Mikey said, struggling with the large slender package.

"I'll help," Jane said jumping up from her spot on the floor.

"Easy," Pete cautioned. The two kids set the gift in front of Faith, then scrambled back to their Legos.

She eased the wrapping off, catching her breath when she uncovered a beautiful framed drawing that she instantly recognized as Pete's work.

"Oh, Pete. It's beautiful." Tears pricked her eyes as she saw the drawing he'd made of her and Jane. "I absolutely love it."

"I'm glad." Pete looked a bit embarrassed. "I wasn't sure what else to give you, especially at the last minute."

She was touched by his thoughtfulness. "You're so talented. I'll treasure this always."

She turned to give him a hug, and their embrace quickly turned into a warm Christmas kiss.

"Your daddy is kissing Mommy again," Jane said.

"Maybe it's your mommy who kissed my daddy," Mikey argued.

Faith pulled away with a sigh. "We kissed each other, okay? I thought you wanted to play with your Legos."

Thankfully the kids were easily distracted.

Faith glanced over at the drawing Pete had made of his family, then back down at hers. "What if I asked for another drawing for next Christmas? Maybe one that included all four of us."

Pete went still, his gaze searching hers. "All four of us? You, me, Mikey and Jane?"

"Yes." She held his gaze. "I care about you, Peter. Very much. And I know it's too soon for you, but maybe in time, you might consider a drawing that included all four of us. Together."

As a family. But she didn't voice that wish out loud.

To her surprise, Pete let out a laugh. She frowned. "Why is that funny?"

"I'll be right back." He bent and gave her another quick kiss before getting off the sofa and heading upstairs. Bemused, she tried to understand what he was doing.

He returned a few minutes later with a second drawing. One that featured all four of them.

Together. As a family.

"I wanted to give you this, but worried it was too much, too fast." He set the framed drawing next to the first one. "Faith, I love you. Very much. We can take our time, there's no rush, but I don't want to imagine a future without you and Jane."

She loved the way he included her and Jane, together. "I love you, too," she confessed.

"Faith." Pete pulled her back into his arms and kissed her. This time, they ignored the giggles of their children.

"Merry Christmas," he whispered.

"Merry Christmas." She rested her head in the crook of his shoulder.

This was God's plan for them. Beautiful, wonderful, Christmas blessings.

* * * * *

Dear Reader,

Christmas is a very special time of the year, one in which we should always remember our blessings. It's been an honor and privilege to work on this series with such a talented group of authors.

I hope you enjoyed Faith and Pete's story, along with the entire True Blue K-9 Unit series. I've spent time in New York, but not necessarily in Queens, so please forgive my mistakes, as they are truly my own.

I love hearing from my readers, and can be found through my website at www.laurascottbooks.com, on Facebook at Laura Scott Author and on Twitter, @laurascottbooks. I also offer a free novella for all newsletter subscribers. If you're inclined to participate, you can join through my website.

Yours in faith,
Laura Scott

CRIME SCENE CHRISTMAS

Maggie K. Black

For Penny, Judy, Garfunkel, Simba and Teddy.

For the Son of man is come to seek
and to save that which was lost.
—Luke 19:10

ONE

Every spare inch of computer expert Danielle Abbott's little corner of the NYC K-9 Command Unit in Queens, New York, glittered with Christmas cheer, from the array of smiling snowmen who lined the shelf over her desk to the tiny strings of sparkling lights she'd hung up over her evidence board.

She leaned back in her chair and stretched her hands above her head, linking her fingers together and sending myriad bracelets jangling down her arms like bells. It was a quarter to seven at night, six days until Christmas, and already a small pile of cards and little gifts had begun accumulating on her overcrowded desk. All week long, officers and their K-9 partners had been dropping by to help themselves to both human and canine holiday treats, as well as invite her to join them for celebrations over the holidays.

Truth be told, she wasn't sure how many of the invites were because her colleagues loved her ability to input just the right thing into exactly the right programs to find them that one perfect frame of security footage or rare scrap of data to solve their cases. And how much of it was the general feeling that the command unit's resident cheerful spinster shouldn't be alone at this time of year, especially among those friends who'd been around her long enough to know she'd been engaged once, to a man who'd broken her heart two years ago on Christmas Eve.

Whatever the reason, it sure was nice to be thought of as a part of the team.

She pushed her glasses up higher onto the bridge of her nose. Today they were red with tiny green sprigs of holly on the arms, and she was as blind as a bat without them. She leaned over her desk, switched off the last of her three computers and did a quick lipstick check in the screen before standing up. The lipstick was also red—a bright and shiny gloss—as was the color of the tasseled scarf she wrapped three times around her neck. 'Twas the season after all. She slid her coat on and yanked the alligator clip from her hair, letting her long blond curls tumble down around her like a cape. It was only then that she scooped her tote bag up off her desk, intent on tossing it over her shoulder before heading out into the night.

An envelope fell out. It was plain and brown, with no markings to show where it had come from. Two words were printed on the front in bold, block letters: *Please find—*

The words were followed by a black squiggle, as if the writer had been about to write something more but was interrupted. Questions cascaded through Danielle's mind like text on a screen, like who was this from and how had it gotten into her bag? But none of those compared to the question of *why?* Why was there no more information? What could they possibly be hoping for?

Presumably she'd somehow managed to sweep it up with other things off her desk, because the idea of anyone else having the gall to touch her bag, let alone slip something inside it, was unthinkable. But why would anyone think it was okay to just drop work on her desk without talking to her and creating a proper evidence trail?

She opened the envelope and looked inside. There was no letter, no note, just a single four-by-six-inch photograph of a little girl, who was maybe about eighteen months old, standing on a beach in a bright rainbow bathing suit and pigtails. A shiver ran down Danielle's spine.

Who was she? What kind of trouble was she in?

Please find...

The message was so simple and so direct, it was almost as if the words had actually been written by a child.

She slid the envelope back into her bag and started for the door, saying a few quick goodbyes as she went. But still the cryptic words and little smiling face filled her mind. Crimes involving kids were some of the most heart-wrenching. The most satisfying, too, though, when they had a happy ending. And, yeah, she knew she should probably leave the picture on her desk to deal with in the morning. But somehow, something about the girl's smiling face made Danielle want to keep her photo close.

Whoever she is, Lord, and wherever she is, please keep her safe and help me find her.

She stepped outside, and the chaos of the streets enveloped her. Thick snow pelted down, landing in puddles of slush at her feet. People huddled with their heads bent low as they brushed against each other on the busy sidewalk. Bright displays and Christmas greetings assailed her from shop windows on all sides. Night had fallen hours ago, leaving the city aglow in the hues of artificial lights.

She ducked down an alleyway, taking one of her favorite shortcuts through the familiar maze of streets and narrow alleys that would take her home to the small room she rented in the apartment of a married NYPD couple and their teenaged sons.

Something clattered behind her in the darkness. She paused and glanced back, feeling every muscle in her body tense. But there was no one there. Okay. She pulled her tote bag closer to her side. Her steps quickened. Clearly the mysterious and unsettling envelope had put her on edge. She wasn't sure why. Was it the innocence of the girl's face or the knowledge someone had slipped the picture into her stuff without telling her? Was it the word *please*? She didn't know. All she knew was that her heart was racing as if she was running from someone or something and didn't know what.

Lord, why is this troubling me so much? Help me crack this, whatever it is.

Footsteps sounded behind her. She spun back. A man rushed at her, wide in a puffy ski jacket. A ski mask covered his face.

Help me, God!

Her hand dived into her bag, feeling for her mace, but she wasn't fast enough. The mugger's hand barreled into her chest like a linebacker's, knocking her back so hard against the wall she felt herself smack against the brick. Her glasses slipped from her face, leaving behind nothing but indistinct and hazy shapes, as suddenly she could only clearly see a couple of feet ahead of her. Her fingers brushed the smooth metal cylinder. She felt for the safety cap and flicked it open. But before she could so much as pull it from her bag she heard a click and saw the barrel of a handgun hovering before her.

"Don't move!" The masked man pressed the weapon between her eyes. "And don't even think about screaming."

"Hey, what's wrong?" Officer Teddy Kowalski froze on the bottom step outside the NYC K-9 Command Unit, as

he watched every nerve in his Belgian Malinois K-9 partner's body leap to attention. "Garfunkel! Dude! What's
going on?"

It had only been a few months since Teddy and Garfunkel started training together, but already the two new
recruits trusted each other implicitly. The young tracking
dog looked almost like a slender German shepherd, with
a strong honey-colored body and a black mask of fur that
ran all the way from the tip of his snout to the tops of his
ears that Teddy told him made him look like a superhero.

The connection between Teddy and Garfunkel had been
tight and immediate. The dog had been named for a fallen
officer from Staten Island, Detective Frank Garfunkel,
whose widow was a friend of Teddy's mother. Detective
Garfunkel had been almost like a father to Teddy after
his own abusive father had bailed after a particularly bad
fight with Teddy's then-pregnant mother, something that
had led to Teddy being born prematurely and with multiple
health problems. Garfunkel the dog had excelled in basic
training and proved his mettle just days after graduation
by finding a gun that a criminal had tossed into the snow.

If his canine partner was convinced something was
wrong, then that was good enough for him. Teddy stretched
himself up to his full six-foot-six form and scanned the
street, peering through the pelting snow and over the heads
of the crowd. Lollygagging shoppers and rushed commut-
ers jostled and competed for space on the teeming sidewalk. Snow filled his face, dancing in the streetlights and
obstructing his view. Nothing seemed off and yet, as he
gave the dog's leash a tentative tug, he could feel a strong
resistance. Garfunkel looked up at him. His dark eyes
locked on Teddy's face. The dog whimpered softly.

Garfunkel might be new to this gig, but he'd been
trained well enough to know that he was supposed to ig-

nore things that weren't his business. Whatever was going on, Garfunkel was convinced it was their problem to solve.

What am I missing here?

His phone rang in his pocket. It was his mother's ringtone, not that anyone else really had his personal number. He and Garfunkel lived with her in the small home where he'd grown up. Mom no doubt wanted to remind him of all the stuff he'd promised to pick up on the way home and the things he needed to get done around their small house before the holidays. Not to mention he needed to drive her to a pre-Christmas holiday dinner party tomorrow at the retirement home where a widower friend of hers from church lived. The dog's whimpers grew louder. The phone kept ringing. He knew without a doubt which one his mother would tell him to deal with first.

"I hear you." Teddy's ran a hand over the dog's head. "Someone's in trouble. Let's go."

The dog howled, a long, deep sound that rose like a horn signaling battle. Then he took off running, pulling Teddy after him as they pushed their bodies through the crowded streets.

They rounded a corner and he heard the faint sound that Garfunkel's exceptional hearing had no doubt picked up. Someone was screaming. The noise was muffled and faded into the noise of the street so well he wasn't surprised civilians hadn't heard it or that those who had hadn't paid attention. The dog pulled him to an alley. His barks rose to a furious protective howl, as if he was taking whatever was unfolding personally. Teddy pulled him to a stop at the end of an alley, unholstered his weapon and stepped slowly forward. Garfunkel growled softly.

"Stop! Police!" The words flew from his lips even as his eyes were still adjusting to the darkness. And then he saw what exactly his partner had alerted him to. Two figures were trapped in a struggle down at the other end of the alley, their forms half obstructed by garbage cans and falling snow.

A mugging? An abusive boyfriend? Something worse?

"Back off!" a man shouted. "This doesn't concern you. The lady and I are just going to go have a little talk." *A talk? About what?* "Just turn around and walk away."

"You know I can't do that!" Teddy called. And Garfunkel wouldn't have let him if he'd tried. "Let her go."

Slowly, Teddy strode deeper into the alley, weapon at the ready, praying the sound of his voice and the dog's growls would be enough to de-escalate whatever was happening. The figures grew clearer. There was a tall man in a puffy black jacket and ski mask, pinning a woman up against a wall. Her hair tumbled around her shoulders. Then the man yanked her around, gun at her temple, so she stood like a human shield between the criminal and the cop. Teddy's heart froze as his eyes met hers, free of the thick-framed glasses she usually wore. It was Danielle, the intimidatingly brilliant and beautiful computer tech, who'd so generously doled out treats to Garfunkel earlier.

Nobody messed with a friend of Garfunkel's.

"Leave. Her. Alone!" Teddy shouted. He raised his weapon even as he felt Garfunkel tugging at his leash to go save his friend.

"I have a gun!" Cold and calculating menace pulsed through the man's voice. "You and that mutt take one more step toward me and I will shoot her!"

Could Danielle even see him without her glasses on? Walking away wasn't even a question. The dog's barks rose and echoed through the alley. Could he afford to drop the leash at this distance? Would the man get off a shot before Garfunkel reached him? "Drop your weapon! Now!"

He couldn't be sure of a clear shot, not at this distance

and with Danielle's body in the way. It was a hostage situation in a narrow alley, with snow falling in sheets. Garfunkel was a tracking dog. It was nothing they'd ever faced before. One wrong move and Danielle could die.

"I mean it!" the man shouted. "Not one more step. Just turn around and walk out, or I will kill her!"

Help me, Lord, what do I do?

"Hey, Officer!" Danielle shouted. Courage and tears battled within her shaking voice. "What are you waiting for? I'd rather get shot in this alley than dragged off by some creep. So, unleash your dog and take him out!"

TWO

Could the officer hear the fear in her voice? Did he recognize who she was? She didn't even know which one of her colleagues the cop was or even if he was someone she'd personally worked with. Since the mugger had knocked her glasses off, the cop was nothing but a very large blur to her, with a snarling and barking blob at his feet.

"Last warning!" The officer's voice boomed. It was familiar and spoke of protection and strength. "Drop the weapon and let her go, or I'm unleashing the dog. I'll give you to the count of three. One."

"Don't do it!" the criminal shouted.

Danielle closed her eyes.

"Two!" The cop's voice sounded.

"I'll shoot her! I mean it!"

Save me, Lord!

"Three!"

A bullet ripped the air beside her head; it took her a breath to realize the mugger fired past her toward the dog. Barking echoed deafeningly around her. The mugger let her body go and yanked her tote bag from her shoulder, so fiercely she felt her knees buckle beneath her. A bolt of fur and fury shot past her. She tumbled to the ground. A pair of strong and warm hands reached for her, one taking her arm and the other supporting her back. She gasped a breath, willing her wobbly legs to please stop shaking long enough to let her stand. Barking faded in the distance.

"Hey, Danielle, it's okay." The officer's voice surrounded her, gentle, strong and above all reassuring. "He's gone. You're safe."

She knew that voice. *Officer Teddy Kowalski?* The face that swam before her eyes was a soft blur, but the sound of his voice rang a bell somewhere deep in her core along with the memory of a tall and broad man, with a kind and shy grin, whose determined dog had dragged him past her desk six times in the past four days looking for pats and treats. She looked up at the cop who now held her in his arms. "Teddy?"

"Yeah." A smile filled his voice. "Yeah, it's me. I've got you."

"It was just a random mugging." She wasn't sure if she was saying that out loud for his benefit or to reassure herself. "I was just in the wrong place at the wrong time."

"Mm-hmm. Now, let's get you back up on your feet."

Well, that had been a noncommittal sound if she'd ever heard one. She reached for him and gripped his strong arms with her gloved hands as he helped her to stand. "Where's Garfunkel?"

Teddy chuckled slightly. The gentle laugh seemed to envelope her. "He took off after the guy."

"Shouldn't you go after him?" she asked.

"Yeah, but I'm not just going to leave you here alone. Are you okay? Did he hurt you?"

"I'm fine," she said. "He just took my tote bag."

She raised her chin, hating as she did so to realize how much it was quivering. Her voice was coming out shaking and squeaky too. *Come on, Danielle!* She was a New Yorker. It hadn't been personal. The mugger hadn't known who she was or targeted her personally. Somehow telling herself that helped. Although it would be even more helpful if Teddy would say it. What could he possibly think of her falling apart like this?

"I think he served time in prison," she said, forcing her mind to focus on facts and not the helpless emotions swirling around inside her. "I caught sight of a tattoo on his wrist between the cuff of his glove and the end of his sleeve. I didn't get a good look but judging by the faded color and crudeness of it, I think it was prison ink. Thankfully, I left my laptop at the office, so he didn't get any police work or information about cases I'm working on. My keys and wallet are still in my pocket too. So all I'm out are my gym clothes, some makeup, loose change and a couple of romance novels. I'm good."

She was determined to be. Yet, as she pushed herself back to her feet, she felt her legs wobble. His hand steadied the small of her back.

"Hang on," he said. "Give yourself a moment. Here, let me help you find your glasses."

"They've probably fallen into my scarf. It wouldn't be the first time I'd dropped something in there."

"Let me." He let go of her arm, hesitated for a moment, then his fingertips touched the skin at the side of her neck and she realized he'd taken his gloves off. "You're right, here they are."

She felt him brush the hair back from her face. Then he helped her slide her glasses on and everything came into focus. She looked up. A face came into view, with kind blue eyes, a jaw that was somehow both soft and strong, along with a tall, broad form that somehow made her feel small but safe.

She couldn't remember the last time anyone had made her feel either.

"See? You're all right," he said.

His hand stayed on her back. Her fingers lingered on his arms for a long moment. And neither of them let go.

Woof! A triumphant and muffled bark sounded through the alley. They leaped apart and turned. Garfunkel trotted toward them with his tail high and his ears perked. There was something clutched in his mouth. It was her bag.

"You got it!" she called. "Way to go, Garfunkel!"

She bent down toward the dog. But he stopped in front of Teddy and sat.

"Good dog," Teddy said. He reached out. "Drop it." The K-9 dog dropped her bag in front of Teddy. "Thank you." He ran a quick hand over the dog's head, ending with a scratch behind his ears. Then he turned and gave the bag to Danielle. "I'm sorry. It probably has teeth marks and slobber on it."

"No worries," she said. She took it from Teddy and then stroked Garfunkel's side. "I'm just happy to have it back."

Teddy reached for his radio.

"Wait!" she said. Her gloved hand landed on top of his. "What are you doing?"

"I'm calling it in."

"But it's just a random mugging and I'm fine."

His head tilted to the side, reminding her of Garfunkel. "You can't possibly know that. He could've been trying to kidnap you. He could've targeted you because you work for the NYPD. Either way, I'm not in the habit of ignoring the fact that crimes have been committed or someone who needs me."

Someone who needed him? Who said she needed him? Yes, he'd been there for her. He and Garfunkel had saved her life. But that didn't mean she was about to collapse into his arms... Well... She wasn't about to let the fact that she'd already literally collapsed in his arms mean she was going to do it again.

"Well, I'm not in the habit of letting other people take care of me." Maybe that wasn't quite how she'd wanted to put it, but those words were out now so she'd let them stand. She started to look through her bag. "And I wasn't going to suggest we do nothing. I'm going to go back to work, file a report myself and then go through security camera footage in the area to see if I can get a clear shot of the guy. Then I'll cross reference it against former cons who've served a long enough prison sentence they might've gotten a tattoo. If all goes well, I can identify him and have police waiting to greet him when he gets to wherever he's going."

She heard Teddy clear his throat, like he was debating whether or not to say something. But she didn't look up. Instead, she focused on her bag. It was all there. Her gym clothes, her makeup, her books... *Oh, no!*

"What's wrong?" Teddy asked.

"I had a picture of a missing child in here," she said, "and now it's gone."

Garfunkel trotted by Teddy's side as they walked back through the NYC K-9 Command Unit to Danielle's office, his head held high and his tail wagging. Teddy figured he felt pride at having helped his friend and happiness at knowing he was probably going to get another treat. Between the dog biscuits and enthusiastic welcomes, Teddy suspected that Garfunkel was beginning to develop a bit of a crush on the computer tech. Not that he could blame him. Danielle Abbott was an undeniable head-turner, with a way of walking into a room that made everyone automatically sit up and take notice. Her technological skills were second to none. She was absolutely brilliant.

Right now she also seemed upset and didn't want to talk about it. Was she rattled by the attack? Was it the fact that although Teddy and Garfunkel had searched the snow and followed the mugger's trail until he'd lost it in a parking lot, she hadn't been able to find the picture that was missing from her bag? Was it both? Either way, when he'd tried to ask she'd brushed him off. Now, all he could do was wait and see if she'd open up.

And pray.

Thankfully, due to Garfunkel's keen nose, they'd recently made a large drug bust at the port. So his schedule was clear of active investigations for the next few days while he wrapped up a few miles of paperwork. With Christmas days away, and Danielle was clearly dealing with something, it looked like the timing couldn't be better.

"All right, let's get to it." Danielle set her tote bag on her desk, snatched two doggie treats from a tin and dropped them into Garfunkel's waiting mouth, and then switched on the power bar behind her computer. Christmas lights dazzled, dancing angels swayed and a spinning carousel of tiny horses began to spin. She sat down with her back to him. Her fingers flew over her computer keyboard. Garfunkel waited another hopeful moment, wagging his tail, but when no more treats arrived, he lay down on the floor between them.

Teddy chuckled under his breath and was glad Danielle knew how to set limits. If it was up to Garfunkel he'd have eaten the entire tin.

Teddy's phone buzzed in his pocket and Danielle's eyebrows rose, just a little, although her face didn't look away from the screen. It was his mother again. He texted her back quickly, telling her he was running late, then he slid his phone into his pocket and sat down in a chair behind Danielle.

He had absolutely no doubt his mother would understand. A former professor of economics, Doctor Peg Kowalski was a warrior who'd earned her PhD and taught college while raising him on her own. An avid gardener too, his mother had been an absolute force of nature until two hip replacements, arthritis and a stroke had forced her to slow down.

He couldn't imagine what it was like for his mother to be dependent on somebody else to pull the weeds from her garden or pop downstairs to grab something from the basement. Or what it had been like for her, decades earlier, to study for her degree while sitting beside her infant son's hospital bed not knowing whether Teddy would even make it through the night. His friends and colleagues who lived at home all saw it as something temporary, just until they found the right job, got married, saved enough money and "grew up."

It wasn't like that for him, and never could be, even if it meant delaying pursuing a romantic relationship and the start of a family of his own. Sure, there were probably a few kindhearted and attractive women out there who wouldn't blink at the thought of spending their lives in a little house on Staten Island with him and his mother. His mother and her friends had tried setting him up with a few. But he'd never gone on more than an awkward and failed first date with anyone, let alone had his heart feel a twinge.

In fact, the only time he'd ever felt his heart come anywhere close to twinging was the weird way it'd frozen in his chest when he saw Danielle at the end of the barrel of that thug's gun.

"Okay, so I've got multiple scans running to see if there's any security footage I can get of the alley and the surrounding streets," Danielle said, her eyes locked on the screen. "I've sketched what I can remember of his wrist tattoo and run it through our criminal database, but that's more of a long shot. And I sent a quick email blast to everybody working here to see whose case the missing child is. Hopefully, whoever's case it was will get back to me tonight, tell me who she is and be able to get me another copy of her picture."

Hang on, he thought—she'd had the picture of a missing child in her bag but didn't know who she was or even which cop was assigned to the case?

"How do you not know who the missing child is?" he asked.

"I found the picture in my bag," she said, "with no details about where it had come from, except for the words *please find* printed on the outside of the envelope. I'm guessing someone dropped it on my desk and I accidentally scooped it up, because the only places I've been besides work today were Griffin's for coffee and Papa's Gym for their lunchtime aerobics class. Honestly, the entire thing is unusual."

He'd say so. What reason could anyone possibly have for not giving her more information to go on than that? It was like something a child would write. Or someone desperate and in a hurry.

"How old was the child?" he asked. "Was it a boy or girl?"

"It was a little girl, maybe eighteen months old. She was wearing a rainbow bathing suit and standing on a beach. Do you know of any open cases about a missing child that young?"

He shook his head. "No."

"Well, hopefully another cop does."

"Anything distinctive about the beach that might help us narrow down the location?"

"Not that I can remember." She went back to typing.

"And before you ask, no, it's not possible somebody gave it to me and I forgot."

"I wouldn't ever dare suggest such a thing," he said. "Is it possible somebody put it directly into your bag?"

"Possible, but unlikely. I mean why would someone do that?"

He could almost hear the gears turning in her brain.

"Is it possible that's what the man who attacked you was after?" he asked.

She paused for a long moment. Then he heard her voice, so quiet it was barely above a whisper. "I really hope not."

THREE

Teddy watched as Danielle took a deep breath and raised her hands high above her head, linking her fingers as she stretched. He wondered just how hard she was working to focus on doing her job and keep her own fears at bay.

"Hey," he said softly. "It's okay. You'll figure it out."

"I hope so," she said. "The professional in me knows it's not my fault that the case doesn't have a proper paper trail, but..."

"But?"

She turned back toward him. "But...my heart can't stop thinking that somewhere out there is a little girl, who's scared and away from her family at Christmas."

She wiped a tear from the corner of her eye, lifting her glasses and smudging her makeup. Suddenly he felt himself rolling his chair across the space between them, swerving around Garfunkel as he went.

"You'll find her," he said. "I know you will. I have un-limited faith in you. And I'll do everything I can to help."

His hand reached into the empty space between them. She reached back, and for the briefest of moments he felt her fingertips brush against his. Something like an electric current moved through his limbs, both shaking and strengthening him at once. Then she sat back and so did he.

"You're right," Danielle said. "Nothing stays truly lost forever. Some things just take time to find."

She spun toward the computer and he heard her whisper a prayer for the child's safety under her breath.

"Amen," he echoed.

She glanced back, just for a moment, but long enough for him to see the smile that curled at the corners of her lips and the light that sparkled in the depths of her eyes. Then she turned to the screen and he watched as she worked. Windows opened and closed in front of her. Security camera feeds rolled from multiple angles. Emails pinged, were quickly checked and then shut again. It was like watching a musician at work. No, more like watching a maestro conduct an entire orchestra. Finally she sighed, twisted her locks up in a knot at the back of her head and let them fall.

"Eighteen officers have responded to my email so far," she said, "which is good for this time of night. None know anything about a missing child case that matches that description or the picture. As for the mugger, all I've got is a fuzzy shot of the back of the guy's head. The only reason I'm not brushing this off instantly as a random mugging by a repeat offender is the fact that the picture's gone." She tilted her head to the side. "Also, I can't believe you're still here."

"Why is that?" he asked.

"Normally, I can't work with somebody looking over my shoulder. But you're really quiet. Well, calming."

Good. The thing about being a big guy was it was pretty easy to be intimidating without meaning to. He'd never wanted to add being loud to that.

"It's a good quality," she added.

He felt heat rise to the back of his neck. "I'm just sorry you didn't find out more about the picture."

"Thanks," she said. "Sometimes all I can do is set things

in motion and wait for results to come in. But I always find what I'm after eventually."

She got up and wrapped her coat back around herself. He and Garfunkel stood in unison.

"Do you want a ride home?" he asked. "Garfunkel and I have a long drive ahead of us back to Staten Island. At this time of night the bridge is going to be jammed, so we're better off waiting a bit."

Besides, he didn't exactly like the idea of her walking home alone.

"Thanks." She flung her scarf around her neck. "But I'm only about a twenty minute walk from here."

Garfunkel's ears perked.

"We'd be happy to walk you."

"It's okay. I don't need an escort."

"I know," he said, quickly. "But Garfunkel would never forgive me if I made him miss out on an opportunity to walk you home. He's heard us say the word *walk* twice now. Do you really want it on your conscience that you told him you were taking a walk and didn't invite him?"

Garfunkel wagged his tail hopefully. Danielle laughed.

"Okay, fine, you guys can walk me home," she said. "But only because Garfunkel should really get some exercise before you make him sit in a vehicle all the way back to Staten Island."

"Deal." He'd take it.

She shut down her computers, he clipped the leash on Garfunkel and they stepped out of the command headquarters into the night. They walked side by side through the busy streets, so close to each other that their shoulders kept touching. She pulled her hood over her head and random blond curls slipped out, framing her face. He wondered if anyone had ever told her how beautiful she was, and if so, just how much courage a man would need to even try.

"Are you going to move closer to work?" she asked. "So you won't have to commute? I hate driving and can't imagine what it would be like to be stuck in a car for an hour each way instead of getting to walk to work."

He changed the subject. "Who are you spending Christmas with?"

"I haven't decided yet," she said. "My parents are on a cruise. We'll celebrate a late Christmas after they get back. A few different friends here have invited me over, and my church is having a potluck. There's a ton of stuff going on."

"Sounds busy," he said. For a moment, the thought of inviting her to come to Christmas with him and his mother crossed his mind. But how could he possibly ask her to give up several far more interesting events to trek for over an hour, on one of the busiest days of the year, to play Scrabble with him and his mom?

"How about you?" Her voice cut into his thoughts.

"My mother," he said. "It's just her and me, and Garfunkel, of course. We're still living in the same small house she's had since I was born."

"And how is your Christmas shopping going?"

"Terribly," he admitted. "I haven't even started yet, which is pretty bad considering I'm only buying gifts for Mom and Garfunkel."

"This is me," she said and stopped walking, and he realized they'd reached a doorway that led to a block of apartments overtop a row of stores. "The family I live with has a place on the second floor. I'm going to the Columbus Circle Holiday Market tomorrow night after work. If you've never been, it's pretty spectacular. It's all outdoors and there are all kinds of stands selling amazing homemade things. The NYPD Police Band is playing at six. You and Garfunkel are welcome to join me for the show. I'm sure you'd find some great presents there. There are some really nice food stands too, if you'd like to grab dinner after the band plays. I could fill you in on anything I manage to find out about the picture between then and now."

He felt a slow smile cross his face. "Thanks. I think Garfunkel and I would really enjoy that."

"Say…by the stage at quarter to six?"

The grin on his face was matched by the light shining in her eyes.

"Sounds good." His phone rang in his pocket and her back suddenly straightened in a way that reminded him of how Garfunkel leaped to attention whenever he sensed danger. Now what was that about?

"Excuse me," he said. He fumbled for his phone, pulled it from his pocket and answered it. "Hi, Mom."

"Teddy, hi." Peg Kowalski's voice came through the phone. "I'm just calling to let you know the plow came by and piled up snow at the end of the driveway. You'll have to park around the corner and dig your way in."

"Thanks for the heads-up." He frowned. By the looks of things he'd also have to add shoveling the driveway to his to-do list tomorrow, along with chopping wood, taking his mom to her holiday party and the shopping he'd meant to do today. All things that had somehow managed to slip his mind. So much for taking in the holiday market with Danielle tomorrow. "I'll be on my way soon. Just walking someone home."

"Is she pretty?" Peg asked. She was only teasing him. It was a wild guess on his mom's part that the person he was walking home was female, but this time she wasn't actually wrong. He didn't know how to answer. Danielle Abbott was attractive in a way the word *pretty* didn't even begin to describe. He ran his hand over the back of his neck again, this time sending wet snowflakes down his collar, and didn't answer. Peg laughed. "I'll take that as a yes. See you when you get home."

They said goodbye and hung up. He slid his phone back into his pocket and looked at Danielle.

"That was my mom," he said, just in case she hadn't caught it. "I had told her I'd be home by now. Also, I'm really sorry but I don't think I'm going to be able to make it to the market after all."

"Ah, okay," she said. Her eyes dropped to the snow at their feet. "Well, thank you for the walk and all your help."

"No problem," he said. He looked down at his feet too. "I really would like to come to the holiday market tomorrow. I just can't. It's one of my last days off work before Christmas and I promised to help my mom with a bunch of stuff. I'm sorry."

"No problem." Danielle nodded slowly. She rubbed her hand over Garfunkel's head, then she dug her keys out of her pocket and opened the door. "Thanks again, Teddy, for everything. I'll see you around the office."

He felt his hand twitch, wanting to reach out into the empty space between them. He wanted to tell her that being invited to join her tomorrow at the holiday fair meant a lot to him, that he really liked her and that spending that little bit of time walking with her had been the highlight of his Christmas so far. Instead all he said was, "Good night, Danielle. Keep me posted with what you find out about that missing girl. And if you ever need anything call me, okay? Anytime. Day or night. Can I give you my number?"

She slipped through the door. "Don't worry. I know how to find your work number if I need it. If I don't see you before then, have a Merry Christmas."

"You too." But the words had barely finished crossing his lips before the door closed between them.

* * *

People had mothers they needed to take care of and Teddy hadn't been brushing Danielle off, he'd just forgotten he had stuff to do, she told herself firmly as she wove her way through the dazzling stands and displays of the Columbus Circle Holiday Market. It had been almost a full twenty-four hours since Teddy and Garfunkel had charged to her rescue in the alley and still she couldn't get the officer's face out of her mind. At the corner of 59th Street and Columbus Circle, steps from the subway and Central Park, the maze of crafts, decorations, creative arts and gourmet foods was one of her favorite things about spending Christmas in the city. But so far even that hadn't been enough to get her mind off the embarrassing way she'd blurted out the invitation or how Teddy had turned it down. At least she hadn't let it distract her from her work, even if she hadn't gotten any closer to finding out who the little girl was, where the picture had come from or who had mugged her for it.

She pressed through the market. The smells of cookies, apple cider and hot chocolate filled the air. Carolers sang near the giant glowing outdoor tree. Families and couples strolled between the stalls. This to her was Christmas, the bustle of people from all different walks of life coming to celebrate peace on Earth. Events like this were one of the reasons she couldn't imagine ever living anywhere else. So why then did her mind keep flitting to the blue eyes and warm smile of the gentle giant who lived on Staten Island?

She checked her phone. It was almost six. She cringed to remember the feeling of suspicion that had swept over her whenever she heard Teddy's phone ping, wondering if he was telling the truth about who was on the other end. She'd thought she'd gotten over how her ex-fiancé, Gil, had made her crazy, hiding his affairs by claiming it was his mother on the phone or his grandmother he was rushing off to see. By the time the entire relationship had crumbled down around her at a Christmas Eve party, two years ago, she was left with no idea just how many times and ways he'd lied to her and just how many untruths she'd believed.

Never again. Her career was built around cold, hard facts. Her personal life would be too.

"Excuse me." The words flew from her mouth automatically as someone bumped into her hard from behind. She spun around, with her hands raised, just in time to see a figure in a dark ski jacket and winter hat pulled down so low she couldn't see his features. He disappeared into the crowd before she could catch a glimpse of his face. A shiver ran down her spine.

Come on, Danielle. You live in New York. People bump into you all the time.

The place was beyond crowded. There was no reason to be worried, let alone rattled. Yet she'd been on edge ever since the day before. The memory of the cold metal gun pressed up against her skin hadn't left her once. Neither had how helpless she'd felt. Or the picture of the little girl who still needed to be found.

Lord, I can't imagine what she's feeling right now. Please help law enforcement find her and get her home for Christmas.

She bought two small packages of fudge, one peanut butter with candy canes and one dark chocolate, and said a quick "Thank you and Merry Christmas" to the dark-haired girl and her mother behind the table. Then she moved on down one aisle and up the next. Her phone buzzed in her pocket. She stopped and reached for it. It was Ian Bell, manager of Papa's Gym and by far the most encouraging and supportive athletic instructor she knew. Ian was twenty-two. His father, Chester—aka Papa—had run the gym until his recent retirement and the death of his wife. Danielle prayed for Ian and his twenty-year-old sister, Hailey, facing their first Christmas without their mother.

"Ian! Hi!" Danielle held the phone to her ear with one hand and sheltered it with the other to block out the noise around her. "What's going on?"

"Hey!" Despite his usual enthusiastic and booming tone, thanks to the noise of the market she could barely hear Ian's voice. Danielle moved toward the end of the row and slid around the corner into the quiet no-man's-land down at the end of the stalls, sheltered by a long row of flapping tarps to keep out the wind. "I was just calling everyone to make sure you knew we were having our final class before the holidays tomorrow. Two o'clock, with food and drink afterward."

"Yeah, I'll be there." The bakery stall that she'd passed earlier flitted across Danielle's mind. "How's Hailey doing?" Danielle asked. "I haven't seen her around much."

The slender college student with a fondness for children was studying to be a nursery school teacher and frequently ran Papa Bell's kids' program and babysitting room.

"She hasn't been well," Ian said. "Her stomach tends to bug her a lot when she's stressed."

Danielle could all too sharply remember how painful her first Christmas after breaking up with her fiancé had been. She couldn't imagine how hard the first Christmas after losing a parent was.

"Well, if there's anything I can do, let me know," she said.

"Will do. Thank you."

They ended the call. A motion to her left made her glance toward the end of the aisles. A tall man was standing down at the end of the opposite row. Not shopping or browsing, just standing. He was wide with a bent nose, small, narrow eyes and a scowling face, and while she didn't recognize him she couldn't shake the feeling he'd been staring at her.

Was it the same man who'd bumped into her earlier? Or the man with the prison tattoo who'd attacked her the day before?

She walked quickly down to the end of the stalls, cut through an aisle and wove her way back through the shoppers until she came out by Central Park. She glanced back. The man was nowhere to be seen.

Her phone began to buzz. Another call was coming in. She didn't recognize the number, but her heart leaped with the no-doubt foolish hope it could be Teddy.

She answered. "Hello?"

"Danielle Abbott." The voice was male, deep and dripped with menace as he said her name. "Listen to me very carefully. You will forget about the girl in the picture. You will stop trying to find her. Or I will be forced to kill you."

FOUR

Fear gripped her heart like a vise. For a moment her fingers felt so numb she thought she was about to drop the phone.

No, a little girl's life was in danger. Somewhere the girl from the picture was waiting for someone to find her and bring her home for Christmas. Danielle would not let her down.

"Who are you?" Danielle asked. She gritted her teeth and willed her voice not to shake. "Where's the girl?"

The man didn't answer. She quickly opened a separate window and ran a trace on the number. Her heart sank. It was a disposable burner phone. Once she got off the phone she might be able to trace where it was sold and what cell tower the call pinged off of. But for now, if she kept him talking she might find out more about the child.

"You've already been to jail at least once, right?" Danielle asked. "This doesn't have to end badly for you. Just let us come get the girl and take her back home to her family."

The man with the prison tattoo still didn't answer. She wondered if he was conferring with someone else. Did he have an accomplice?

"Just tell me, is she okay?" Danielle pressed. "Is she

hurt? Please, just let me talk to her and make sure she's okay."

She closed her eyes and tried to listen for other voices or background noise. But all she could hear was the whistling of the wind and the sounds of the fair. Her eyes darted around. Was the man here? Was he at the fair? Did that mean the little girl was there too? Surely anyone who'd kidnapped a child wouldn't be foolish enough to bring her out somewhere public where she could run away or be spotted. Unanswered questions tumbled through her mind.

"How long has she been with you?" she asked. "How did you know I was looking for her?"

No answer. She closed her eyes and prayed. *Help me, Lord. What do I do?*

"Who are you?" she demanded. "What do you want?"

"I want you to leave this alone." The voice was back. "The girl is safe. She is at home, where she belongs, with her family and the people who love her." The reassuring words clashed with the cold and merciless tone in his voice. How could she possibly believe a word of that? "I'm not the bad guy here. I'm just looking out for the kid and her family."

"Then let me talk to her," Danielle said, fighting with every question for any scrap of information or data she could glean, no matter how small. "After all, she's a toddler and practically still a baby. It's not like she's going to be able to tell me where she is or who she's with. I just want to hear her voice and know she's all right. Some proof she's even still alive."

"You are going to drop this."

But how could she? The little girl's face filled her mind, so young and hopeful in her rainbow bathing suit, and the two words scrawled on the envelope: *Please find.*

Physical fitness and athletic ability had never been

Danielle's strength. She knew she didn't have the ability to chase down an armed criminal, tackle and fight them to the ground that so many of her colleagues had. She'd never had either the coordination or stamina of the women she exercised alongside at the gym. And her aim had never been all that great with a gun.

But she knew how to gather and examine evidence, pick it apart for holes and question everything. And if the person who'd somehow slipped her that picture had been looking for someone to tenaciously grab hold of this mystery and not let go until they'd solved it, then they'd chosen the right gal for the job.

"If you know who I am," Danielle said, "then you know I'm not the kind of person who's about to take some strange, anonymous and threatening man's word for anything. If you want me to drop this, then give me the evidence and information I need to believe you." Or slip up and give me what I need to find this girl, rescue her and get her back home where she belongs.

"I'm not about to back down or stop looking for this girl while there's even the possibility she's in danger. So if she's safe, prove it. If you've got nothing to hide, stop threatening me from the shadows. If she really is with her family, then tell me where she is and let me talk to her family. But until then, as long as there's even a possibility that somewhere out there is a little girl who's lost, scared and away from her family at Christmas, I will not stop looking for her and trying to help her."

Her entire body was shaking now from both fear and courage clashing like two waves inside her. She just hoped her voice sounded a lot more determined and brave than she felt.

"No, you listen to me," the man said. His voice was even colder now. "This isn't a negotiation. This is a warning.

You will stop looking for the girl in the picture. You will make no efforts or attempts to find her. You will stop now and forget you ever saw her picture. Do you understand me? Because if you don't, I will kill you to keep her safe."

Her body shook, and her knees buckled. The phone went dead.

Something bumped into the small of her back.

She screamed, her hands flying up protectively toward her face as she spun backward.

And nearly fell over Garfunkel.

"Garfunkel, no!" Teddy exclaimed as he watched the beautiful tech guru practically tumble over his dog. "Get back!"

Teddy jumped forward, reaching for Danielle and catching her with both hands, feeling her weight land in his arms as she steadied herself. When he'd reached the holiday fair, spotted Danielle and noticed she was on the phone, he'd hung back, waiting for her to finish. Garfunkel, however, had no such manners. The dog had eagerly lunged to the full end of his leash and butted her in the back.

"I'm so sorry!" Teddy said. "I guess Garfunkel still needs some training for his manners. Usually he only head butts me."

"Thank you," Danielle said. They stood there for a moment, with his hands clutching hers and Garfunkel standing in between them. She was shaking. "You're here."

"Yeah." When he'd been talking to his mother that morning, he hadn't been able to help himself from mentioning Danielle. He just couldn't get her off his mind, especially as he felt like he'd blown it when she'd invited him to join him at the holiday fair and he'd had to shoot her down. His mother had urged him to blitz through everything that needed doing and suggested he drop her off early for the Christmas party at the retirement home so she could help her friend Ned with setup—and he could still join Danielle. His mother had even said she'd catch a rideshare or taxi home if need be—which wasn't an option as far as Teddy was concerned.

Still, it had been very kind of her. Especially considering he'd been planning on sticking around for the party in case his mother needed him. Between the scars left on her face by his father long ago, her physical limitations from the arthritis and the fact that her speech was still slow and slightly slurred from the stroke, Teddy didn't exactly like leaving her places with people he didn't know. Too many of them overlooked her or presumed her mind wasn't sharp and didn't see the amazing woman his mother was on the inside. No, it was his job to look out for his mother just like she'd looked out for him. But she'd practically insisted he meet Danielle.

"My plans changed," he said.

He felt a slight whimper and looked down between their hands to where Garfunkel was leaning against her legs.

"You're shivering," he added. "Are you okay?"

"No." She shook her head, and he watched as tears formed in the depths of her eyes. For a moment it was only the fact that Garfunkel was standing between them that kept him from pulling her into his arms. "He called me."

Teddy didn't need to ask who *he* was. There was only one person he knew of who could've filled her with such fear. He glanced around. There were people everywhere. They needed to find somewhere to sit and talk.

"The man who attacked me called my cell phone from a disposable burner phone," she said, her voice so low it was almost a whisper. "He threatened me. I tried to get him talking and to put the little girl on the phone. I tried to find out anything I could to get more information from him… And I got nothing… When I get back to my computer I can try to use cell tower data to figure out roughly where he was when the call was placed, but that can't happen until I get back to my computer and it could take a lot of time. I also thought someone might've been staring at me earlier, but I don't even know if I'm right about that…"

His spine straightened to alert much like Garfunkel's did when the dog sensed danger.

"Do you see that person now?" he asked.

"No," she said. He watched as fear, frustration and helplessness washed over her at once. "I had the man on the phone, Teddy, and I didn't get any leads to help us find her. I blew it."

"No, you didn't." He squeezed her hands. "Just because you didn't solve the crime in one phone call doesn't mean you blew it. Don't you start beating yourself up now. Please, Danielle. You've already done more than anyone could've expected you to. Let's find somewhere to sit. Okay?"

"Okay." She nodded. He dropped one of her hands but kept hold of the other one tightly. They walked over to an open area, away from the crowd, that was set up with benches and freestanding heaters that glowed with dancing blue and orange flames. She sat down, and he sat beside her, feeling the soft wool of her gloved hand tucked inside his leather-gloved one.

Garfunkel sat down directly in front of her, pressed his body against her legs and laid his head on her lap. She ran her other hand over Garfunkel's head, stroking the soft black mask of fur between his eyes and running her fingers over his ears. Yeah, Garfunkel had good ears for that. The dog looked up at her with large and worried eyes. Teddy imagined his own looked much the same as he gazed at the fierce and unexpectedly fragile woman now sitting beside him. Teddy sat there for a moment, holding her hand tightly in his and wishing there was something more he could do or say.

"Do you mind if I go grab us a hot chocolate?" Teddy asked. "Warm drinks are good for the nerves and there's a stand right over there, just outside my peripheral vision, and it's kind of calling me."

She looked up at him now. A smile crossed her lips. It was faint, but also real, and he'd take it. "Yeah, that would be great. Thank you."

He smiled.

"Back in a second." He stood slowly, and he glanced down at Garfunkel. "I'm leaving you in charge. Stay here and guard Danielle for me, got it?" Garfunkel woofed and pressed himself closer against Danielle's legs. Danielle chuckled softly. Teddy leaned down and brushed a hand over his dog partner's flank. "Good dog." He pressed the dog's leash into Danielle's fingers. "I'll just be one moment."

He walked to the refreshment stand and bought drinks for them both, feeling something tugging his eyes back to Danielle with every step. Thick flakes of snow tumbled down from the sky around her. Gentle light from the fire danced across the lines of her skin. Her gaze was fixed on Garfunkel's face. As he watched, she unwound the red scarf from around her neck and tied it around Garfunkel in a stylish side knot. The dog sat up straighter and his tail thumped the ground. Danielle laughed. Did she have any idea the effect she had on him? No, probably not. He couldn't even explain it himself. He paid for the drinks and walked back.

"I'm amazed how good Garfunkel looks in your scarf," he said. "He looks almost proud of it."

"Well, the hood on my coat is so huge I didn't really

need it," she said, "and there are so many dogs around here in little Christmas coats, I thought Garfunkel might like to look a bit more festive."

How he loved her playful sense of humor.

And it was hard to argue with that. Especially considering the happy thumping of Garfunkel's tail. "Yeah, you wouldn't want him feeling left out."

"Exactly," she said, "and I think it looks even better on him than it did on me."

"I wouldn't go that far," Teddy said. He handed her a hot chocolate, then sat beside her, reached into his pocket and pulled out a folded piece of paper. "Also, I jotted my personal phone number down for you. Thought it would be good to exchange numbers. So, next time we'd know how to reach each other."

"Thank you," she said. She took it from his fingers and slid it into her pocket. "What happened to your plans for tonight, anyway?"

He wasn't sure what to make of the tone of her voice. It was almost like she was about to whip out a police notebook to jot down his answer.

"They changed," he said. "I thought my mom needed me tonight, but it turned out she didn't. Garfunkel was all in for going to the fair from the get-go."

He'd been hoping for a smile, maybe even a laugh. Instead she just nodded.

"Tell me about the phone call," he said.

"There's not much to tell," she said. Already her voice was stronger and more steady. She pulled out the phone and held it up for him to see. "The number is a randomly generated one assigned to a burner phone. I won't be able to trace it. If he's smart, he'll have ditched it already."

"You kept him talking for almost six minutes," he said,

feeling something like awe move through his voice. "That's a really long call for a threat."

"I hoped if I kept him talking he'd give me something I could use," she said. "But I got nothing. Not even proof she was still alive."

He reached for one of her hands and squeezed it.

"Hey, you did the absolute best you could, I'm sure of it," he said. "Let's take a deep breath and then tell me what you do know."

He watched as her chest rose slowly and fell. Then he felt her hand squeeze his back.

"He told me that the little girl was safe, where she belonged, with her family," Danielle said. "His tone was cold and hard. But his words made it sound like he thought he was protecting the girl. He told me if I didn't stop trying to find her he'd kill me."

The last part sent shivers of fear running down Teddy's spine, combined with a fierce, hot, instinctive desire to protect her. He clenched his jaw and focused on thinking like a cop.

"Did you believe him?" he asked. "About his motivations?"

She scrunched her nose for a minute, making her glasses bob up and down as she thought.

"Maybe," she said. "It's such a bizarre claim for him to make. So, I think he believed it, even though it's clearly nonsense. Because if the little girl really was safe and with her family, then he wouldn't have stolen her picture and threatened my life."

Yeah, he liked how her mind worked.

"Well then, you have gotten us new information we didn't have before," he said. "She might've been kidnapped by an estranged family member or someone who's convinced himself he's family."

She was nodding now. The tears were gone from her eyes. She took another sip of hot chocolate.

"There's something else we know now too," she said and sat up straight. That same look he'd seen in her eyes when she'd been searching the computer screen filled her gaze. "He knows I'm looking for this little girl and thinks intimidating me personally will stop the investigation. He didn't threaten the NYPD. He called me personally. What if that means this isn't an open police investigation? All this time I thinking that someone somewhere had to know about this case and I just hadn't managed to find it yet. What if she was never reported missing? I'm the only one who's seen this little girl's picture, knows she's been taken and is looking for her."

FIVE

"Well, if so, then whoever slipped that picture into your bag came to the right person," Teddy said, "and not just because you've already alerted the entire NYPD, but because you're determined, tenacious and driven—not to mention insanely good at your job—and if anyone can find her, you will."

"Thank you." She pulled her fingers away from his and ran both hands through her hair. "But if I'd realized it was possible I was the only one who knew about the picture I'd have made a copy of it and kept it somewhere safe. Now, all I can do is try to recreate it from memory. Thankfully I have a really good forensic artist program on my laptop I can use to do a police sketch of her picture. Also, I need to revisit everywhere I went yesterday in case there's a possibility the picture didn't come from work. I got coffee at Griffin's and did a quick aerobics class at Papa's Gym. It's theoretically possible someone slipped the picture into my bag in either place."

Possibly, but who would just slip the picture into her bag? Why not file a missing child report? Why not go to the police?

But even before he could ask the question she was dialing her phone.

"Hey, Danielle!" Carter Jameson's warm voice came down the phone line. The former K-9 officer had recently taken over Griffin's diner after being injured in the line of duty.

"Hey, Carter! How's Rachelle?"

"Good, good."

Carter and the tenacious reporter had fallen in love while he was working a case over the summer and were now engaged to be married.

Teddy discreetly sat back to give her privacy for the call. But Danielle gestured him closer and held the phone between them so that he could listen in.

"I'm here with Teddy Kowalski and Garfunkel." Danielle's voice was suddenly all business. He'd always liked how she was direct when there was a job to be done. "I'm putting you on speakerphone. I don't know if you've heard through the grapevine but I'm looking into a case about a missing girl."

"Yup," Carter said. "News travels fast around here. Let us know if there's anything we can do."

"Maybe." Danielle quickly filled him in on the details of the past twenty-four hours. "It's possible that someone slipped the picture into my bag at Griffin's. People know it's a cop hangout."

"Can't think of anything out of the ordinary from yesterday," Carter said. "But I'll talk to the staff. I can also put up a notice on our bulletin board."

"Do it," Danielle said. "Keep it simple and short. Information sought regarding a picture of a missing girl. All tips will be kept in strictest confidence. Then give them my number. Also add they should call the crime hotline if they have knowledge of a crime."

"Got it."

Her life had been threatened and here she was giving out her personal number? Didn't she get how risky that was?

"I'm also going to do a sketch of what I remember her picture looking like," she said. "I'll be sending that around later."

"Sounds good," Carter said. "We'll be praying."

They ended the call.

"Are you sure about putting yourself out like that?" Teddy asked. "You're basically putting a target on your head."

"There's already a target on my head." She tossed her hair around her shoulders. "Whoever has kidnapped the little girl already has my number and knows how to get to me. He wants me to shut up, go away and stop trying to find that girl. But my doing that doesn't help her. It just helps whoever took her."

She stood up and rolled her shoulders back. Did she have any idea how impressive—even intimidating—she was? Probably not.

"I want to talk to the manager of Papa's Gym too," she said. "But I'll wait to do that in person. I don't know the manager, Ian Bell, very well. His mother died just a few weeks ago and this is his and his sister Hailey's first Christmas since her death. But I like them. He's only twenty-two and yet since taking over the reins of the place from his father a year ago he's run the place like a pro. I just need to be more careful there. Griffin's is different. Carter is part of our NYPD family."

"Is it possible that Ian had anything to do with this?" Teddy said. "Speaking as a cop, he sounds like a potential suspect. He's strong and charming, but you don't know much about him. He has access to your phone number and has just gone through a tragic loss."

"Except I just told you that I don't think it's him." Danielle bristled. "I don't like thinking I could be wrong about someone."

He had no idea what to say to that.

"So what do you want to do?" he asked.

She smiled, suddenly, like she really appreciated the fact that he kept asking her questions.

"I want to be smart about this," she said. "Especially as the only proof I have that a child is even missing is a picture I no longer have in my possession and the fact that I was threatened. There's a Christmas party at the gym tomorrow. We can go and ask some discreet questions. As I said, I'd rather talk to Ian in person about this. For now, my next steps are to go home, grab my laptop and do my best to recreate the girl's face from memory. There was also the face of the man I thought might've been staring at me earlier. I'll sketch him, as well."

"Those are great first steps," Teddy said.

She nodded. "Yeah, I think so too."

"How about we have dinner before you head home?" he asked. "I haven't eaten yet and the original plan had been to meet here and grab food."

The bridge of her nose crinkled as she thought. It was cute.

"I want to get on this right away," she said. "How about we pick up some food here and head back to my place? We'll have the living room to ourselves. We can eat and work at the same time."

"Yeah," he said, feeling a grin that was so wide he suspected it looked goofy spread across his face. "I'd like that."

"Me too." Her smile deepened and for a moment they just stood there smiling at each other.

"I just need to check in with my mother first," he said. "She's at a party with a friend. I don't really want to go into the whole thing but it's possible she might need me. Hold on."

"Is there something wrong with your mom?"

He didn't know how to answer that. His mother was an amazing woman, but if he wasn't there to have her back people tended to dismiss her, and so he liked checking in to make sure she was okay. That was the truth. But it also opened up a whole bigger conversation he didn't want to have right now and could lead to her asking questions he didn't want to answer. He didn't want to have to explain that his mother had visible scars that had come from his father or how Teddy was committed to always being there for her, even if it meant never moving away from home. He opened his mouth, hoping it would somehow come up with something to say to allay the doubt now flickering in Danielle's eyes. When it didn't, he reached for his phone.

He'd somehow missed six text messages and three phone calls from his mother. She'd gotten slightly dizzy during the party. Nothing serious, but while she thought everything seemed fine, the medical staff at the retirement home were now insisting she rest in their on-site clinic awhile for observation, which meant she was missing dessert. Could he please call the retirement home, speak to the staff and fill them in about her medical conditions and what medications she was on?

This was what he'd been afraid of. He never should've let her go alone.

"Look, I'm really sorry," he said. "But something just came up. I need to make some calls and might have to go pick up my mother. I don't think I'm going to be able to do the dinner and brainstorming thing after all. But I can at least take you home. Just hang tight for a couple minutes. Stay right here and you should be safe. Nobody who's trying to stay hidden is going to attempt something in a crowd like this. I'll be back in a few."

He'd done it again. Teddy had gone from *yes* to *no* so fast it had given her heart whiplash. She turned away from him and closed her eyes. No, she couldn't afford to start overanalyzing why Teddy kept making plans and breaking them. It was like her brain was a supercomputer and it would be a mistake to let it try to use up all her processing power on the wrong thing. Teddy was clearly an unreliable person who had a lot going on in his life that he didn't want to talk to her about. She couldn't let herself lose focus over that, or take it personally, despite the mixture of embarrassment, disappointment and doubt swirling around inside her heart.

Lord, please help me take charge of my feelings right now. I need to calm my heart. I need to switch off whatever it is that's making me feel this way and stop hurting over this.

She turned back to where she last saw him and Garfunkel a moment ago, expecting to see Teddy standing there with his back to her and his phone to his ear. Instead, she'd completely lost him to the crowd. Despite the fact that he'd given her his number, texting him to ask where he'd gone was out of the question. At least not until she'd lost sight of him for a lot longer than a few minutes. She'd spot him and Garfunkel again any second. But although logic told her that he couldn't be far, months of her ex-fiancé's excuses and sudden disappearances had left her with a scar on her heart that was still healing.

The past does not dictate the present, she told herself firmly. Some things took time. Especially healing. The fact that Gil had been a liar and a cheat didn't mean that Teddy's flakiness was something she needed to feel hurt about. But still, the damage her ex-fiancé had done to her sense of confidence and self-esteem was pretty deep.

She'd thought she was going to spend the rest of her life with him, that he just had a demanding work schedule and that a good girlfriend, a good fiancée, would be understanding. But his habit of making and canceling plans had left her on edge. She'd never really known where she'd stood or if she was seeing him from one night to another. She'd get all dressed up for a party only to get a phone call while she was on her way there telling her he was stuck at work. Or she'd make them dinner, only to have him show up three hours late and tell her he'd already eaten. When she'd finally stumbled in on him with his arms around another woman at a Christmas Eve party two years ago, she'd already been so used to his excuses and lies she didn't know what to believe.

Her pastor had told her that healing from that would take time, and that when she was finally ready to risk her heart on love again, both she and the man she gave her heart to would have to work through the emotional remnants of Gil's betrayal together.

If so, she needed a man far more steady and reliable than Teddy to work through it with. And Teddy deserved a woman a lot less broken than she was.

The snow was falling thicker and faster now, dancing in the wind. She raised her eyes to the dark sky above and watched as huge flakes swirled down. Then she closed her eyes and felt them gently hit her face. But despite the fact that they weren't a good fit romantically, she couldn't deny the fact that Teddy Kowalski was still amazing. He was kind, sweet, smart and definitely someone she would've liked to have gotten to know better. There was something solid, comforting and grounding about having him there.

The connection between him and Garfunkel was something special too.

But clearly she wasn't ready for a personal relationship with anyone and neither was he. He might be an incredible cop, but he was hardly the only cop she knew. Maybe she'd be better off finding someone else to work with on this case. Someone who was equally good at his or her job, without any added complications.

Her phone buzzed in her pocket. She pulled it out. The number was unfamiliar. Fear pounded through her heart as her eyes scanned the holiday fair for Teddy. Was it the man who'd threatened her? Was he calling her back from a different burner phone?

Lord, if it is, help me hear what I need to hear and say what I need to say.

She took a deep breath. "Hello?"

For a moment she couldn't hear anyone on the other end. She started walking through the stalls, searching for Teddy.

"Hello?" She tried again. "Is anyone there?"

"Hello?" The voice was female and hesitant. "Is this Danielle Abbott?"

She exhaled. "Yes."

"I need your help to find my little girl."

SIX

Danielle felt every nerve in her body leap to attention. A lead! She actually had a lead. But where was Teddy? Her footsteps quickened, and she scanned the stalls as she went. Surely he wouldn't have just left.

"Hello? Are you still there?" The woman's voice was so hesitant it was almost stilted.

It was also oddly familiar. But Danielle couldn't quite place it. She ran a quick trace on the phone number. Sure enough, it was another burner.

"Yes, I'm here." Danielle started for a quieter spot at the edge of the holiday fair. "Sorry, it's a little noisy where I am right now. But I'm listening and I will help you find your little girl. Do we know each other?"

Another pause spread down the phone line. Danielle waited and prayed, feeling her brain shift into focus as she did so.

"You got the picture of my daughter?" the woman asked, ignoring Danielle's question. "You're looking for her, right?"

"I saw the picture of your daughter," Danielle said carefully, deciding not to tell her for now that she'd been attacked by a man who'd threatened her and stolen it, for fear of spooking her caller. "I want to help you and I will do whatever it takes to help you find her. But I need more information. Can we start with her name? Or yours? How long as she been missing?"

She pressed her lips together, feeling her chest ache for this woman, whoever she was. But feelings would only get them so far. She needed facts. She needed something she could take action on.

"I can't tell you that," the woman said. "It's not safe."

Okay. Danielle had analyzed enough tip-line calls to know people calling in about crimes often gave vague or even unhelpful information, because they were too upset to think straight. The wind whipped more sharply. Danielle pulled her hood tighter over her head, wishing she hadn't playfully given her scarf to Garfunkel.

"Okay, then how about you start with something simple?" Danielle suggested. "When did you put the picture in my bag?"

"I'm sorry," the woman said. "I can't tell you anything. Not over the phone."

Again, there was something about both the tone of her voice and her hesitant way of speaking that was so very familiar.

If only she could figure out where she'd heard it before.

"Hey, it's okay," Danielle said. "We'll take this slow and figure it out. Just tell me what you can."

The wind was picking up, making the canvas of the booths flap around her and sending shoppers shrieking and scurrying. There was way too much noise for her to even hope to make out the woman's voice clearly let alone pick up background sounds to try to figure out where she was calling from. Danielle's pace quickened as she searched the stalls in vain for Teddy.

Where was he?

"Do you promise to help me find my daughter?" the woman asked.

For a moment the threatening voice from the phone call flickered through her mind along with the memory of the gun pressed between her eyes. She was risking her life. And yet, the thought of saying no never occurred to her.

"Yes," she said. "I promise I will do whatever it takes to help you find the little girl and bring her home safely."

"Okay, then I'll meet you somewhere and we can talk. But only if it's really public, you come alone and promise not to follow me when I leave."

"Okay," Danielle said. "I can stick to that as long as we find somewhere that we both feel safe." That meant no cars or vans, back alleys, empty businesses, parking garages, vacant lots or private homes. "Where do you want to meet?"

"There's a large diner," the woman said, "called Penny and Judy on the Upper East Side."

Danielle let out a breath she didn't realize she was holding. Yeah, she knew the place. It was a good choice. It was very public and open, with good lines of sight, great visibility on all sides and well-placed exits. There was no way either of them could be ambushed by anyone and it was exactly the kind of place it would be safest for both of them to meet.

"I'll be there in twenty minutes," the woman said.

Danielle blinked. "No, I need more time than that. I might not be able to make it there that fast."

"It has to be now," the woman said. "I can't come later and I can't stay long."

"Why?" Danielle said. "Are you in trouble? Will someone notice you're gone?"

No answer. Danielle frowned. Twenty minutes was barely doable but not ideal. She could make it if she caught a cab or cut through Central Park. But it would give her limited time to call the NYPD and get someone to meet her there for backup. A cop, someone in plainclothes, who'd hopefully stay undetected but cover her back.

Like Teddy would have, if he hadn't disappeared.

"It has to be now," the woman said again. "I'm being watched. I can't be gone long. If they get suspicious they'll hurt her."

"Got it," Danielle said.

"I'll be there."

The line went dead. Danielle blew out a hard breath. She didn't like it. She didn't like it one bit. But she'd completely lost Teddy and if she didn't act fast the woman might not show up at all. She allowed herself one more quick glance around the holiday fair, hoping against hope that she'd spot the tall and handsome officer and his loyal sidekick. But Teddy and Garfunkel had seemingly disappeared.

She glanced around for a cab, and when she didn't see one she turned and started quickly through the park, skipping the wide main walkways and cutting through narrower side paths between the trees to get there faster and looking for more privacy in order to be able to call Teddy and explain the situation without being overheard by anyone. She pulled the piece of paper Teddy had given her from her pocket, entered the number and dialed. The call went through to voice mail. She hung up and tried again.

Snow swirled heavier, the wind picked up and she pulled her hood tighter over her head. Trees hemmed her in. She tried Teddy again. The call went to voice mail again. This time she left a message. "Hey, Teddy, it's Danielle. Sorry to disappear on you, but I got a tip. The little girl's mother called wanting to meet—"

The blow came from her right, hard and knocking her forward before she could even see the man who'd dealt it.

Her glasses tumbled from her face, catching on the cord around her neck. She stumbled back up and swung, feeling her hands claw ineffectually at the damp fabric of a ski mask. Then a large gloved hand clamped over her mouth as a second grabbed her by the hair and yanked her backward into the bushes. A cold voice filled her ears.

"I warned you to leave this alone," he said. "I told you to forget about the girl. You've left me no choice. You're coming with me."

Frustration burned at the back of Teddy's neck. He'd taken so long trying to sort things for his mother that Danielle had finally given up and called him, twice, and he'd been stuck letting it go to voice mail. He imagined her sitting by the freestanding heaters, surrounded by the crowd and getting impatient waiting for him. There'd been so much noise in the fair around him, he and Garfunkel had been forced to take shelter behind a stall just to hear the people on the other end of the phone. He'd spoken first to his mother, who'd done her best to assure her son that she really was okay. Then he'd gone through two different employees of the nursing home before finally getting hold of his mother's friend Ned. Teddy had spelled out the medications his mother was on one letter at a time. He got that everyone there was just trying to take care of his mother. But well-meaning or not, the staff were clearly frustrating her. She was smart enough to know how she was feeling and if she was strong enough to go back to the party. He couldn't imagine how upsetting it was for her to age, knowing she could do less and less, and then on top of it to be treated like she couldn't think and make decisions for herself.

He crouched down lower inside the stall and pressed his finger to his ear. He could feel Garfunkel's eyes on him. Yeah, he knew. He'd left Danielle for far longer than he'd intended to. The fact that she'd called looking for him made him feel even worse. At least he knew she was somewhere safe.

"I use a car service," his mother's friend Ned was saying. "I can take your mother home tonight after the party."

Yup, that's what the plan had been earlier in the day. But that wasn't the plan now.

"Don't worry about it," Teddy said. "I'll come pick her up. I'll be a little over an hour."

"You don't need to hurry." His mother was back on the phone. "I'm fine now."

The voice mail alert from Danielle's number flashed again on his screen.

"The party's going to go late," his mother added, "and Ned is happy to make sure I get home."

Ned was also in his late sixties and needed a walker. Sure, Teddy had been cautiously okay with the idea of her catching a taxi when they'd made plans for tonight, but that was before his mother's dizzy spell.

"Don't worry," Teddy said. "I'm going to head over there as soon as I can. It might take a while, depending on traffic, but I'll be there to pick you up when the party's over. I'll call you back in a bit. I've got to go take care of something first. If you need me again, just call."

"Okay, kiddo, love you."

"Love you too, Mom."

He ended the call and checked the voice mail, his frustration at hearing Danielle had left to chase a lead without him turning to panic as he heard her voice cut off followed by what sounded like the phone hitting the ground. He ran out into the fair, even as he pressed the callback button on his phone. Her phone rang through to voice mail and Danielle was nowhere to be seen. He scanned the area, striding quickly with Garfunkel by his side, searching the stalls for her. Why had she left the safety of the crowd? He looked down at Garfunkel. The dog's eyes were locked on his face.

Gently he untied the knotted scarf from around Garfunkel's neck just enough to wave the tip before the dog's nose. Not that he thought Garfunkel needed any help remembering her scent. "Garfunkel, where's Danielle?" he asked. The dog's head cocked. "Go find Danielle!"

The dog barked and took off running through the market and across the busy street, with Teddy hanging on to the end of the lead. Garfunkel bounded into Central Park, pulling Teddy off the main path. Teddy's heart sped faster.

Lord, wherever she is, and whatever's happened, please help me get there in time.

They pressed on, running through the trees. Then he saw the footprints and the broken branches littering the ground. There were signs of a struggle. Prayers pounded through him. Panic pushed his heart up into his throat. But he barely had time to register it, as Garfunkel pulled him through the bushes.

Then the trees broke and he saw them, two dark figures in the snowy dusk. A big masked man was trying to drag Danielle backward, his hand around her throat as she struggled against him. But Danielle was fighting hard and seeing her there, battling against her attacker, made something leap inside Teddy's chest. He pushed his legs forward, Garfunkel pulling at the leash and howling. He knew the feeling. His own heart was pounding so hard it was like something inside was about to rip his chest in two.

He dropped the leash. "Go get 'em, Garfunkel."

SEVEN

She heard Garfunkel's furious barks filling the air along with the strong timbre of Teddy's voice.

"You won't get another warning," the criminal snapped in her ear. Then he shoved her forward, throwing her into Garfunkel's path even as the ferocious snarling dog leaped for him.

She felt her body collide with Garfunkel's. Woman and dog tumbled together, falling hard. She gasped a breath, felt the snow hit her body and heard her attacker running away. Then she felt a soft and comforting snout nuzzling her face. She rolled onto her side in the snow and brushed her hand along Garfunkel's warm flank. The dog licked her face gently with a single, almost apologetic lick.

"I'm okay," she said softly, burying her face in his fur. "I'm sorry I crashed into you too."

"Danielle!" Teddy dropped down into the snow beside them.

She detangled from the dog's embrace, reached for where her glasses had fallen and pushed them onto her nose. Teddy's worried face filled her gaze.

"You need to go run after him!" she said. "You need to catch him."

"I'm not going to catch him," Teddy said. "He has too

great a head start and once he steps foot out of the park there are too many places he can escape to. Right now you're what's most important and I'm not about to leave your side."

His fingers brushed against her face.

Oh. Something was bubbling up inside her. It was a feeling she didn't know quite how to put into words but still somehow longed to be able to hope for and trust in.

"I put a string on my glasses this time, so I wouldn't lose them," she said.

She hoped her feeble attempt to lighten the mood would do something to break the worry that washed over his expression. But instead, as he reached for her, the depth of emotion that filled his eyes was so strong she had to look away.

How could she have possibly thought that he didn't care about her?

"Are you okay?" Teddy's voice was a soft and low rumble in her ear. She found herself reaching for him, feeling the sturdy strength of his arm under her hands as he helped her to her feet. "What happened? Did he hurt you?"

"He was trying to kidnap me," she said, pushing the words through her shaking voice. "He wanted to take me somewhere. I think he wanted to interrogate me, find out what I know about the girl in the picture before he…"

Before he killed me. The words died on her tongue.

"We have to get to Penny and Judy. It's a diner on the Upper East Side," she said. "Right now. This woman called me and told me that the little girl in the picture was her daughter. She wants to meet me there." She tried to steady herself on shaky legs. "We need to go. Now. I have to meet her in twenty minutes. Fifteen now."

But Teddy just stood there in the snow. "You've been attacked."

"Yeah," she said. But she also didn't want to dwell on that right now. She wanted to focus, get to the diner and find the girl. "He wanted to stop me from looking into this." She stood up straight and tossed her hair around her shoulders, pushing way more determination and bravado through her voice than she felt. "I can't let him win. The woman put that picture into my purse and reached out to me. I can't let her down."

For a long moment Teddy didn't say anything. He just stood there looking at her.

"You're not going without backup," he said eventually.

"Agreed."

"Also, I'm pretty sure it's a trap," Teddy added. "For all we know, the woman on the phone was working with the man who tried to kidnap you, to get you somewhere isolated so he could attack you. If he really was the man you saw in the holiday market, then he knew where you were and which direction you'd be headed." He ran a hand over this jaw. "What can you tell me about the caller?"

"The voice was female," she said. "Hesitant and familiar, but I can't place it."

"Okay, how about this," Teddy said. "We head to the coffee shop together, you go inside, order something and sit at the table. I'll stay outside with Garfunkel and keep watch. If she hasn't called and nobody has approached you in the timeframe she set, we bail."

Her chin rose. "Thirty minutes."

"You can make it thirty-five if you want," Teddy said and shrugged. "This is your operation. But either way, I want to make sure you get home safely." She frowned. "What's wrong?"

"The family I live with left this morning on holiday," she said, "which seemed like no big deal earlier because I'm perfectly fine staying by myself over Christmas. But now with everything that's happened I don't feel quite as safe there as I did before."

"Okay, so that's something we've got to think about too," Teddy said.

She'd been half expecting him to tell her she couldn't stay there alone. Instead, it was more like he'd taken the information in and was processing it. She appreciated that.

They trudged through the snow out of Central Park onto a sidewalk and took a cab to the diner, arriving with two minutes to spare. Teddy seemed lost in thought, and while she didn't know what he was thinking about, there was something comfortable, even comforting, about his silence. While he stayed outside, she went in and sat at a small table and waited, watching the clock. Nothing happened. Her phone didn't ring, nobody approached her and while her eyes darted to the door every few minutes with every jingle of the chimes, she never once saw a woman walk in alone, let alone one who seemed hesitant or was looking for someone.

After thirty-one minutes, she ordered two hot chocolates to go and left. Teddy and Garfunkel were standing sentry outside a store a few doors down, chatting aimlessly with people as they passed and the various dogs whose owners had left them outside while they went in to get coffee. He had his phone in his hand, but he slid it into his pocket the moment he saw her coming.

"How are you holding up?" she asked.

"Not bad," he said. "I mostly went for a bit of guy-who's-rideshare-hasn't-shown-up-yet as my cover with a lot of it's New York, so nobody cares why one random dude and his dog are standing on the street."

She smiled at his attempted joke and pressed the hot drink into his hands.

"Thank you," he said. "How did it go with you?"

"I got nothing," she said. "She didn't call. She didn't show. We're back where we started."

"No, you're never back where you started," Teddy said, and there was a strength to his voice that made her want to believe him. "You have everything you remember about the man you thought was staring at you, the two phone calls and the attack, even if you haven't yet figured out what you know. You'll feel better when you sit down at your laptop and get to work."

"You're right," she admitted. How did he always know the right thing to say? "Thank you."

"I had a thought," he said. "How about we swing by your apartment, grab your stuff and then head back to my house? I talked to my mom on the phone about it while I was waiting for you, and she's happy to have you. Our house is small, but it's quiet, and she's offered to warm up some leftover chili for us." He looked down at the patch of sidewalk between them for a moment and then back up at her face. "How about it, Danielle? Would you like to come home to Staten Island with Garfunkel and me?"

He waited for what felt like the longest moment of his life for Danielle to answer. He debated telling her he'd never invited a woman, not even a friend or colleague, home to meet his mother before.

"Yes," she said, and he was surprised at how his heart leaped with joy at that simple word. "If you're sure it's okay with both your mother and Garfunkel, I'd appreciate not being alone tonight."

Well then. Something swelled inside his chest like his rib cage was suddenly full of helium. The feeling didn't dissipate any as they took a cab back to Central Park to pick up his car, then drove back to her place. He waited as she grabbed a few things and then they took the long drive across the bridge to Staten Island. If anything it seemed to grow stronger. Now he sat behind the steering wheel of his police-issue SUV with Garfunkel curled up in the back seat and Danielle sitting beside him, looking out the window as they inched across the bridge. Was he really about to do this? Was he really about to bring her home to meet his mother? It had all seemed so seamless and second nature to invite her and now the closer he got, the more the tightness in his chest grew.

"My mother has various health problems," he said. "Her mobility isn't great. Her speech is slow. She also has a few scars on her face and arms from years ago, when my father hurt her pretty badly, when she was pregnant with me, before he left us…"

"I'm sorry." Danielle's voice cut into his thoughts. Her hand brushed his arm, and he found himself reaching for it. Their fingers entangled. "That's horrible."

"Yeah." He kept his left hand on the wheel and his right hand on hers. "I never met my father. They divorced when I was a baby. But apparently he was a real piece of work. He beat my mother so badly, I was born prematurely with a ton of health problems. But both my mom and I recovered together. It made us really close and it's partly why I'm so protective of her."

He paused a moment. She didn't say anything. Instead, she just sat there in the vehicle with her fingers moving gently over his.

"My mom is the strongest, most amazing person I know," he went on. "She raised me on her own, put herself through university and eventually became a college professor. She does a ton of work with charity. She's a force of nature. But for my whole life, it's like when people have looked at her all they've seen are her scars. I didn't bring friends over because of it and I cringed at how people stared at her or talked down to her in stores. And now that she has mobility issues, walks with a cane and talks really slowly after her stroke, it's even worse. I know I should've told you that earlier, but I didn't know how and I really don't like talking about it."

He could feel that old familiar tension rising up his back, but somehow the fact that Danielle was still holding his hand helped.

"Again, I'm sorry I disappeared for so long in the market," he continued, telling her about his mother's friend Ned inviting her to a party at his retirement home and what happened there. "She needed my help and it just took a while to sort out. I'm sorry."

"It's okay." She squeezed his hand and then she pulled hers away. Her eyes flitted to the darkness outside. "You have nothing to apologize for."

Again he had the feeling that there was something there, something bothering her that she wasn't telling him. They exited the bridge, onto the island, and then he was driving through the old familiar streets back to the small house he'd known as home for his entire life. He pulled into the driveway, walked around to the side of the vehicle to open the door for Danielle, but only got halfway around the vehicle before she'd climbed out. He noticed his mom was pretending not to watch them through the curtains.

Okay, showtime. He was just about to introduce the woman he had a secret crush on to his mother.

They crossed the driveway, he opened the front door and they stepped inside.

"Mom? I'm home," he called, then smiled as his mother's face appeared around the corner of the stairs at the top of the landing. "Mom? This is Danielle. Danielle, this is my mother, Peg Kowalski."

"It's really nice to meet you," Danielle said, quickly taking off her boots. She walked up the steps and reached for his mother's hand. "Thank you so much for your kind invitation."

He stood back in the doorway of his own home and watched as his mother showed Danielle around the main floor of the house and then led her into the kitchen, where a pot of chili was bubbling on the stove. Then he sat with them at the small wooden dining room table, feeling almost like an interloper as Danielle and his mother chatted about the case, the little girl in the picture, the party his mother had gone to that evening and the essential ingredients of a good chili. He never imagined he'd meet a woman he liked who was patient enough to sit through the gaps and pauses in his mother's conversation, who'd appreciate her sense of humor and intensity, who'd see past the outward signs of what she'd survived to who his mother was on the inside.

How didn't I see that Danielle was this special, Lord? he prayed as he poured Garfunkel's food into his dish and set it down for the pup. Maybe he'd always suspected Danielle was that special, but didn't want to get his hopes up that she'd ever look at him twice.

An hour later, he and Danielle sat alone in the basement family room, on opposite couches, with a fire burning in the wood-burning stove. He opened his laptop and started catching up on the drug bust paperwork he had yet to file, thanking God yet again for giving him the time help Danielle.

She opened hers, and for a few minutes there was a flurry of activity as she pulled up various screens, inputted information and sent various searches running. Then, slowly, she sketched out a picture of the girl's face on her laptop. He watched as she worked, her lips pursed and the lines of her brow furrowed in concentration.

"Okay, I think I've got it," she said. "Do you want to come see it?"

"Yeah," he said. He walked over to the other side of the room and knelt down on the floor beside the couch where she sat. She turned the laptop toward him. His breath caught. The girl in the picture looked so young and innocent, with a wide smile and a gap between her tiny front teeth. Two ponytails sprang from the sides of her head. Her eyes glimmered with hope.

"This is her," Danielle said softly. "This is our missing girl."

"You've done an amazing job," Teddy said. "You'll find her. I know you will."

Danielle sat there for a long moment, gazing at the little girl on the screen. Then her eyes closed and Teddy found himself praying for the girl in the picture, Danielle and himself as they looked for her. Danielle whispered "Amen" under her breath and he realized she'd been praying too.

He waited as she went back to her laptop, and for a while silence fell again as she did another quick sketch, flipped through the various programs, looking at results and adding in more information.

"Okay, we've got a mixed bag of results," she said. "Both calls were placed by burner phones, and by triangulating cell tower data I can say they were both made within a mile of the holiday market. So for now, that's a dead end. Also, this is the man from the market." She opened another sketch. A man stared back at him with small eyes, a crooked nose and a cold stare. "I'm going to run him too. Finally, there's this…" She pulled up what looked like a sound wave. She clicked the play button on the screen.

"Hello." A woman's voice filled the room. "I am looking for my daughter. Do you have the picture of my little girl?"

"That's the voice of the woman who called me," Danielle said. Her head shook in apparent disgust. "I knew I recognized the voice of the woman on the phone but didn't know where from. That's because it's not a real person. She's not real. It's a computer-generated voice. The voice that called me, claimed to be the little girl's mother and asked me to meet her was a computer-generated fake."

EIGHT

"For all we know the kidnapper is the one who called me," she said, "to lure me away from the market and test to see whether I'd back down. I went to meet a woman who wasn't even real."

He watched as tears of frustration flooded her eyes, thick and wild, brimming underneath her long, dark lashes and spilling down her beautiful face. Suddenly it was like something burst inside Teddy's chest. He found himself reaching for her and wiping the tears off her cheeks with his fingertips. She threw her arms around his neck and he knelt there, hugging her and cradling her in his arms while she cried into his shoulder.

"It's okay," he said, running his hand along the back of her head. "You will find her. I know you will. You are the smartest, most determined woman I've ever known. I know you're tired and scared, and I don't blame you. Cry as long as you need to. I'll hold you as long as you want and won't let go. But know this, if anyone can find this girl, it's you."

Danielle pulled back and looked at him. But still she didn't let go of him and he didn't let go of her either. Their faces were so close he could feel her breath on his skin.

"But what if I can't, Teddy? I don't know if I can do it."

"I believe in you enough for the both of us," he said. "When it comes to Danielle Abbott and what she's capable of, I don't have a shadow of doubt in my mind. Because you're incredible and if I ever go missing you are one hundred percent the person I'd want looking for me."

She blinked and as her eyes locked on his face something deepened in their gaze.

"If you ever go missing, Teddy, I'll definitely come find you."

"And if you ever go missing, I'll find you," he said.

"Promise?" she asked.

"I promise," he said and felt something deepen in his voice. "If anything ever happens to you, Danielle, I will not rest until I know you're okay."

Her arms tightened around him and they kissed. He didn't know if she'd kissed him first or if he'd somehow gotten up the courage to kiss her. All he knew was that he was kneeling in the basement of his house, pulling the most beautiful woman he'd ever met into his arms and feeling her lips brush against his. For moment they stayed that way, with their arms around each other and their lips gently touching, and Teddy knew he felt more at home than he ever had in his life. Then Danielle pulled away and he sat back on his heels.

Her lips parted slightly as if she didn't know what to say. Neither did he. He just watched as a look that was almost like wistfulness or sadness washed over her face, as if she'd lost something long ago and didn't know how to get it back.

"Are you okay?" he asked. "Was that okay?"

"Yeah, I'm fine." She pulled her laptop up into her arms and held it to her chest. "And you're wonderful. I'm sorry. I'm just really tired."

Oh. He stood slowly.

"My mom has already set my room up for you," he said. "Knowing my mom she'll have gone and dusted all my comic books just in case I missed a spot. Garfunkel and I are going to sleep down here in the basement."

A smile crossed her lips. It was soft and slight, and seemed completely genuine. He stepped way back to give her enough room to stand up without bumping into him. She stood, holding her laptop against her heart like a shield.

"I'm really sorry if I overstepped," Teddy said. "I didn't mean to upset you or put you in an awkward position."

"No, it's okay," she said quickly. "Please don't apologize. I like you, Teddy, a lot. I think you're completely amazing." She paused for one second, then leaned over and kissed him lightly on the cheek. In a gesture that was sweet and kind, but still somehow made his heart sink. "Good night, Teddy."

"Good night, Danielle."

She turned and disappeared up the stairs. He sat down on the couch and listened to the soft murmur of noises filtering down from upstairs as Danielle and his mother talked.

I like you too, Danielle. That's what he should've said. *I like you way more than a lot.*

He liked her in a way he'd never even known he was capable of. He waited until both women had gone to their rooms before he went upstairs himself to brush his teeth. He found Garfunkel lying on the floor in the hallway, across Danielle's doorway, guarding her against anyone who might disturb her in the night. He debated calling to the dog to join him in the basement, then decided he really couldn't blame him for wanting to protect Danielle. So instead, Teddy went downstairs alone, pulled out the sofa bed and lay on it, staring at the ceiling and wondering if Danielle had browsed through any of his books before falling asleep, why she'd seemed sad after their kiss and what he was going to say to her in the morning.

He awoke to winter sunlight streaming through the windows, the sound of laughter upstairs, the smell of coffee and the weight of Garfunkel's head lying on his chest. When he got upstairs he found his mom and Danielle at the table, with his mother's tablet, Danielle's laptop, their phones and what looked like two small turquoise-and-green baubles on the table between them.

"Good morning," he said.

Both women looked up, wished him good morning and smiled. But he couldn't help but notice that Danielle's eyes didn't quite meet his.

"Danielle's been helping me set some stuff up on my phone to prevent the kind of thing that happened yesterday," his mother said. She stood slowly, grabbed her cane and made her way over to the counter. Her hand shook as she refreshed her coffee. "Did you know there's this app that links to all your medications, their side effects and everything? She's set it up so I can share it with Ned and anyone else who asks. I can also use it to order refills. She also signed me up for this rideshare service especially for people with mobility issues and showed me this grocery service too, for when you don't have time to pick something up for me."

Something happy shone in his mother's eyes. He gave her a hug around the shoulders.

"I always have time to pick things up for you," he said, "and sort your medications."

"Well, you shouldn't always have to," Peg said.

His mother walked back over to the table, taking it one slow step at the time. He followed with the coffeepot.

"I've tried to set up apps like that for her before," he told Danielle. "Multiple times."

"I told her," Peg said. "But she's got a way of doing it that works for me. Also, I think she has better ones. And these little green plastic things? They're those emergency trackers you got me. She actually got them linked to that app on your phone. I'm going to leave one next to my chair in the living room and put one in my purse."

Yeah, he hadn't been able to figure them out and it didn't help that his mom had insisted she didn't need them. Teddy glanced at Danielle. "Thank you."

"No problem," Danielle said. "It was the least I could do. I sent the picture to the entire NYPD, and so far no one has recognized her. There are no missing children matching her description in New York or New Jersey. But I've also got a search running of the entire national missing children's database. I'm not giving up hope yet. I'm going to leave multiple searches running on my machine and cast the net a little wider. We might have a hit on the man from the holiday fair." She opened a screen on her laptop and spun it toward him.

The scowling man with beady eyes stared back. "His name is Hal Aberfeldy. He's gone to prison twice on assault charges. Got out four months ago. Nothing in his record notes whether he has any wrist tattoos and I didn't get a good enough look at the man's face in the park to know if it's him."

"And we can't issue a warrant for a man who's served his time just because he might've been looking at you at the holiday fair," Teddy said, sighing through the words as he said them.

"No record of him having a child, but I'm still searching."

"So, what's the plan?" he asked.

"I'm going to Papa's Gym for their holiday party and exercise class." Danielle took her dishes to the counter and rinsed them in the sink. "It's possible someone slipped the envelope with the girl's photo in my bag there. I'm going to talk to Ian and Hailey and make some discreet inquiries. Would you and Garfunkel like to come? Ian loves dogs and the place has a dog-sitting room."

"Sure, sounds like a plan."

He definitely wasn't about to let her go alone. An hour later, they were in his vehicle, with Garfunkel curled up on the back seat and Danielle sitting beside him looking out the window, right back where they'd been a few hours ago, and yet, it was like everything had changed. She'd been in his home and she'd met his mom.

He'd held her in his arms and kissed her.

"I hope everything's okay between us," he said. "If you don't want to talk about what happened last night, I totally get that. I just want you to know that you mean a lot to me, I really like you and if I did something that hurt you, I'm sorry."

For a long moment there was no response and the only sound was the windshield wipers moving back and forth, and Garfunkel's snoring in the back seat.

"I was engaged once," Danielle said. "His name was Gil. Turned out he was secretly flirting and fooling around with a few different women at the health club he preferred over Papa's Gym."

Teddy felt something drop in his stomach like the moment a roller coaster plunged over the edge of a hill. "I'm so sorry."

"Thank you," she said. "It is what it is. We broke up two years ago Christmas Eve. I caught him with another woman."

The pain in his gut intensified. Any man who had even the slightest shot with a woman as incredible, amazing and strong as Danielle and betrayed her was not only a colossal idiot, his actions seemed downright criminal.

"I don't know what to say," he said. "I hate that he did that to you."

"Me too." She turned to face him. "It left my heart kind of raw. You're the first guy I've liked or who's even been interested in me since then, and I guess I don't know how to handle it."

That was honest and he appreciated it.

"Well, if it helps, you're the first woman I've ever brought home to meet my mother or kissed like that. I wouldn't have done that if I didn't really like you." More than liked. "And for the record, a lot of the single guys at work think you're really smart and beautiful. Not just me."

"Well, you're the only one I ever noticed," she said. "But we can't let ourselves focus on that right now. We have to keep our heads in the game if we want to find the girl."

"Agreed."

Even if he didn't know how to stop himself from falling for her.

Papa's Gym was housed in a former warehouse and had the disconcerting knack of looking larger on the inside than it seemed from the outside. Murals of sunny West Coast beaches, palm trees and blue skies covered the walls. A framed picture of Papa Bell, his late wife and their children, Ian and Hailey, hung over the front desk. Right now, half of the main hall had been sectioned off for a holiday-themed exercise class and the other was set up with tables for the potluck. Danielle winced. She'd forgotten to bring food.

"Danielle!" Ian broke away from the crowd and bounded toward them. He was tall and muscular, but despite his imposing frame, there was something about the look in his eyes whenever he taught the self-defense class that had always made Danielle suspect he'd faced more than his fair share of bullies. "So glad you made it! Who's this?"

Ian reached out and ran his hand over Garfunkel's head. The dog sat immediately and wagged his tail. Danielle resisted the urge to point out to Teddy that there was no way Garfunkel would be so happy to meet Ian if he was the same man who'd attacked her. Then Ian reached for Teddy's hand. "Ian Bell, manager of Papa's Gym."

"Teddy Kowalski, friend of Danielle." Teddy shook the other man's hand firmly. Then he gestured down. "Garfunkel Kowalski, dog."

Ian laughed. "Big name."

"He's a big dog," Teddy said.

"German shepherd?" Ian asked.

"Close," Teddy said. "Belgian Malinois."

"Well, it's nice to meet both of you," Ian said. "Danielle can show Garfunkel to our doggy day care. Teddy, can I show you around and introduce you to a few folks, and then you can hop right into our holiday class?"

She wasn't surprised Ian would leap into potential-new-client mode.

"Not a bad idea," Danielle said to Teddy. "Divide and conquer."

"Okay," Teddy said. "As long as neither of us leave the building or go anywhere alone."

Ian's eyebrow rose.

"Teddy's a cop," Danielle explained. "We've been working on a missing child case and if it's okay we'd like to show her picture around and see if anyone recognizes her."

Ian's eyes widened. "Of course."

She dug her phone from her pocket and pulled Aberfeldy's picture up first. "You haven't seen him before, have you? He might have a tattoo on his wrist."

Ian looked down at the picture and frowned. "No, can't say I recognize him."

"You've got security cameras in here, right?" Danielle asked. "What's the possibility of getting a copy of yesterday's footage?"

"So-so," Ian said. "I have about six cameras covering the main areas that feed into the main desk computer. You can have those. But when Papa retired he wired cameras all over the place. I don't even know where they all are. I get the impression he monitors them from his retirement home. Makes him feel like he's still running the place."

"Your father sounds pretty controlling," Teddy said.

"You could say that." Ian shrugged. "He's always been eccentric but it got worse after my mother died. He must've installed even more cameras without telling me after she died, because I went to visit him last week and he pulled up footage of the back room and spent thirty minutes reaming me over how I was slouching."

"Maybe he's lonely?" Danielle suggested.

"Maybe," Ian said. "Anyway, I'll ask him but he might insist on you getting a warrant. You said you were looking for a little girl?"

"We are." Danielle pulled up the picture on her phone. "Have you see her? Could she be the daughter of someone who comes here?"

Ian looked down at the sketch. His forehead wrinkled.

"I don't recognize her," he said. "But she does seem vaguely familiar. Why don't you show her to Hailey? Her stomach's still bugging her, but she didn't want to miss the holiday party. She's in the kids' room."

"Will do. Thanks." Danielle's hand brushed Teddy's as she took Garfunkel's leash from him. "Back in a moment."

Ian led Teddy into the gaggle of people milling around waiting for class to start. Immediately, Teddy pulled out a copy of her sketch of the girl's picture and started showing it around. But still something twisted in Danielle's gut as she watched fellow students flocked around him. Almost all of them were women with the kind of thin and athletic build that Gil had found so attractive.

No, she couldn't afford to give insecurity a foothold. Not right now. She gripped Garfunkel's leash tightly and started down the hall. This was why she couldn't ever kiss Teddy again or think about him romantically. Something inside her was still fundamentally broken. Gil's cheating ways had shattered her self-esteem and ability to trust, and sometimes it felt like she'd never be right again.

The door to the children's playroom was closed, but when Danielle knocked it swung open.

"Hi, Danielle. I didn't know you had a dog." Hailey peeked out the door.

Hailey was a lot thinner than her older brother and almost as tall, with large soulful eyes and dyed black hair. A cheerful toddler was in her arms. Behind her, two older boys, who looked to be about five and six, were playing with cars on the floor. Danielle scanned the room and spotted three separate cameras.

"His name is Garfunkel," she said. "He belongs to my friend, Teddy."

The word *friend* felt odd on her tongue. But what other word could she use?

"Nice to meet you, Garfunkel," Hailey said. She shifted the baby to one hip and reached out to brush the dog's head.

"I'm working on a missing child case right now," Danielle said. She slid her phone out of her pocket. "We're showing around a sketch I did of her."

"Do you have an actual picture?" Hailey asked.

"No," Danielle said. She held the phone up. "Just a

sketch. I did have a picture, but I lost it when my purse was stolen."

As Hailey looked at the sketch, the young woman's face paled, her hands shook and tears filled her eyes.

NINE

Hailey knew something. It was written all over the woman's slender form, from the way her eyes were fighting back tears to the way her hands were shaking.

"Hailey?" Danielle asked softly. "What is it? Who is this little girl? Do you know her?"

"No." Hailey stepped back from the phone like it was a grenade and about to explode. "No, I don't."

"Is it possible you've seen her?" Danielle pressed. "Could she have come here with someone?"

Hailey closed her eyes and took a deep breath. When she opened her eyes again she'd clamped down on whatever had been upsetting her so effectively that Danielle almost found herself wondering if she'd imagined the flood of emotions she'd seen sweeping over Hailey just moments ago.

"I don't know who she is," Hailey said. "I thought for a moment I recognized the girl, but I don't know who she is."

"Yeah, I felt that way too when Teddy showed me the sketch on his phone." Ian's voice came from behind them. Danielle tuned. She hadn't even realized Hailey's older brother had been coming down the hall toward them. "There's something really familiar about her. Maybe somebody else will recognize her."

The baby on Hailey's hip started to cry. Danielle prayed.

Help me, Lord. I feel like there's something I'm missing here. Please help me see it.

"I just came to tell you that class has started," Ian said. "You're going to have to hurry if you don't want to get stuck doing burpees for being late."

Right, that jumping push-up exercise that always made Danielle feel like a flopping fish.

"You go ahead. I'll be right there," Danielle said. Ian jogged back down the hall. Danielle turned back to Hailey. "You have my cell phone number in the gym database. If you think of anything helpful, you can call me, okay? Anytime, day or night, and I'll pick up. I promise."

"Thanks, but I don't know anything that can help you." Hailey reached to close the door. Then she paused with it open a crack. "I hope you find her, though. Whoever she is, I hope you find her."

"Yeah," Danielle said. "Me too."

The door closed and as much as Danielle wanted to push it back open, she knew it would make Hailey even less likely to trust her with whatever she knew or suspected.

Some things take time, she reminded herself. *Nothing stays lost forever.*

It wasn't until she walked back into the main gym area that she realized she'd forgotten to drop Garfunkel off and change into her exercise clothes. There were also over forty notifications on her cell phone, including updates from her own searches and emails from other police officers. She prayed that somewhere in the mix was a good solid lead. She sat down on a bench and ran her hand over Garfunkel's head as he sat down beside her, absentmindedly stroking the dog's ears while scrolling through the list.

Music thumped around her as the class switched from warm-up to high-intensity cardio. She hated missing class.

Although she'd never been all that athletic or coordinated, it was a great way to let off steam and stretch her aching muscles after spending too much time hunched over a computer screen. Teddy seemed to be enjoying the class, though. She watched as he bounced like an enthusiastic and slightly awkward teddy bear in the middle of the exercise floor. His apparent popularity hadn't dwindled any. Helpful students flocked around him, offering to partner with him on exercises and find things like mats and dumbbells as needed.

She couldn't blame them. Teddy was definitely cute. If he stood still in his police blues and stared directly and seriously into a camera, he had the kind of good looks that could see him featured on any police calendar in the country.

But it was more than that. He had this smile that lit up a room. He had a way of both talking and listening that made her want to open up to him. He had this way about him that made her feel safe and accepted, that had made her want to tumble into his arms last night and to feel his lips kissing hers. And somehow, because of it, watching him there with other fitter, stronger and more attractive women buzzing around him made something in her heart beat so painfully she could feel it through her chest.

Her phone buzzed again, with a notification from one of the programs she'd left up and running on her laptop back at the house. The program had found four potential matches for the girl's picture.

She sprang to her feet and glanced at Teddy. He paused, midlunge, and she wondered if he'd been watching her after all. He waved a hand at the class as he jogged toward her. "Sorry, got to go!"

But before he could reach her the fire alarm sounded, loud and piercing, and the sprinklers erupted.

* * *

"Danielle! Are you all right?" Teddy shouted over the sounds of the sirens, as water streamed down from the ceiling above them. Beside him he could feel Garfunkel, immediately at his side, awaiting instructions.

"I've got some new leads," she said, then waved her hands at the pounding sprinklers, "and I don't believe in coincidences."

Around them, people were streaming for the exits.

"We should help," he said, "if we can. But you should stay close. We can't rule out the possibility that someone created a distraction to get you alone and potentially kidnap you."

He reached for her hand, and she let him take it. The main room was almost deserted now. Seemed the gym's evacuation plan had been as effective at clearing the building as the sirens were at nearly deafening him. Water was still coursing from the ceiling, but he didn't catch even a whiff of smoke or fire.

"We're going to do a quick sweep of the building for anyone left behind," he added, "all three of us together. Then we're getting out of here. Can you lead the way?"

She nodded. Her abundant curls were plastered down around her face, sticking to her skin. Determination filled her gaze. And it hit him again just how beautiful she was. "Let's do this."

They ran quickly from room to room, pelting down hallways and pushing through doors, with Danielle on one side of him and Garfunkel on the other. There was no one left inside and no obvious sign of a fire either. By the time they burst out the back door, soaked and shivering, onto the gray snowy street, emergency vehicles had already begun showing up and gym students had dispersed into local coffee shops and stores. Ian was coordinating with arriving authorities.

Teddy located the officer in charge and quickly filled him in on the situation, including the fact that he'd cleared the building. Then he turned to Danielle. Her teeth were chattering and her lips were already turning blue.

"Let's get out of here," Teddy said. "We can warm up and regroup in my vehicle. I've also got a couple of towels in the back and a blanket if you don't mind the fact that Garfunkel's slept on it."

"Garfunkel smell is just fine with me." She glanced around. "I need to get back to my laptop to download those missing children files. But both Ian and Hailey said the girl in the picture looked familiar. Hailey even seemed upset by it. But both said they didn't know who she was."

"Looks like Ian is working with emergency services. Do you see Hailey?"

"Yeah, she's the thin woman hovering beside him."

Teddy looked where she was pointing. Yeah, any conversation they had with her, while she was there, would be far from private. "I'm sure she knows something. But if I try again now I don't think she'll tell me."

"We should wait," he said. "Give her time to think. Maybe whatever leads you've turned up will help guide the questions you ask."

"Agreed."

They made their way to his vehicle, climbed inside and he pumped the heat until they started to thaw. Only then did he start the drive back home.

Danielle flipped the sun visor mirror open and pushed wet strands of hair from her face.

Then she sat back and scrolled through her phone.

"We've gone from having no leads to too many leads,"

she said. "It's going to take me time to download and read through all this data."

His phone pinged, and he glanced at where he'd mounted it on his dashboard. It was a text from one of the women who'd taken his business card at the gym, saying sorry she'd lost him in the crowd.

"You're going to follow up with Ian about the security video footage?" he asked.

She nodded. "Yeah. If he doesn't come through I'll try Papa Bell."

His phone pinged again. It was a different woman from the class inviting him to coffee. He wondered if it was a coincidence or if they'd coordinated their texts to see which one he replied to first. "Speaking of leads."

He chuckled. She didn't.

"Those aren't leads," she said. "You do know that, right? They're to fishing to see if you're free for a date."

Heat rose to the back of his neck. Yeah, he'd suspected as much, but couldn't say definitively one way or another, even though he'd been nothing but all business when he'd been giving out his business card and showing Danielle's sketch around.

"Doesn't mean they don't know something," he said. "I've interviewed plenty of suspects with agendas before. It's part of the job."

"Getting coffee with a beautiful woman who's angling to date you is part of the job?" Danielle asked.

Did he really have to dignify that with an answer? "Don't be ridiculous."

"Don't be naive!" she said and Teddy noticed in the rearview mirror as Garfunkel's ears twitched toward the sound.

"Who says I'm naive?" Indignation rose in his voice.

"What's ridiculous is that you think I'd ever find any of those women remotely attractive!"

"Well, some of them are pretty good-looking."

"Says who?" Teddy asked. "You want to know what I find attractive, Danielle? You. I think you're beautiful. I always have. I think you're something that's way beyond beautiful. You're brilliant, strong-willed, focused and driven. I couldn't begin to tell you if any of those women were attractive or not because the only woman I've ever looked at twice is you!"

His phone pinged again. The first woman who'd texted had sent a follow-up text to ask what he was doing for Christmas. He gritted his teeth and prayed for patience. Danielle still hadn't spoken.

"Look, I'm sorry that your ex-fiancé was a colossally stupid and selfish individual who didn't treasure what he had in you," Teddy said. "I've never actually punched anyone in my life, but when it comes to him I'm definitely tempted to. I get why you flinch every time my phone buzzes. If you need to text me fifty times a day, read through my texts or call me in the middle of the night for me to prove I'm not him, then do it! I'm down for whatever it takes for you to feel safe trusting that the only woman I'm interested in is you."

Please, Lord, help her see how special she is and that all I want is to do is love her.

He swallowed hard. He'd never used that word for his feelings about a woman before. Not even in prayer.

"I know you are," Danielle said. "Because you're that kind of man."

Teddy's heart lurched. "Then what's the problem?"

"I don't want to be that kind of person!" she said. "I'm afraid of being in a relationship again, because I don't want to be the woman who has a panic attack every time a pretty woman notices you or when you have to work late. And I don't want you to turn your life inside out to manage my doubt and worry."

"I don't mind!"

"But I do!" Danielle said. "I have to work. I have to be focused. There's still a little girl out there waiting for us to find her."

"And we'll find her," Teddy said.

He reached for her hand to squeeze it. But she pulled away.

"We will," she said. "But not like this. Not together. I need to find somebody else to stay with until my house-mates come home. I need to find another cop to work this closely with. I'll keep you in the loop on everything and we can coordinate on this case professionally, from a distance. But I can't be in your life like this Teddy and I can't let myself like you this way. We have to end whatever this is and say goodbye."

TEN

Snow buffeted hard against the small Staten Island house. Wind rattled the windows. Danielle sat alone, curled up in a chair and swamped under a pile of blankets, as her eyes scanned the files coming in on her laptop. But her mind kept flicking back to the face of the tall, sweet and strong police officer whose living room she was sitting in.

He and Garfunkel had taken a quick trip to drop Peg off at church. Despite the rideshare app she'd downloaded for Peg, Teddy still felt safer driving her. It would take him less than fifteen minutes, he said, and then they'd have the house to themselves and be able to talk without being overhead. Truth be told, she needed a few minutes alone. They'd barely talked for the rest of the drive back, after she'd broken down and told him they couldn't have a relationship. When he returned, they'd go through the data, find a new partner for her to work with and go their separate ways. Not because of any hard feelings. But because it was what was best for her ability to focus on the case and for them.

Even though the very idea made her heart sink in her chest.

Help me, Lord. Am I doing the right thing? Teddy's

amazing. But he deserves better than someone who doesn't know how to trust.

Her mouse hovered over a missing persons file. She clicked, it opened and her heart stopped as she stared into the same wide-eyed, hopeful smile of the little girl whose picture she'd found in her bag. She grabbed her phone and dialed.

"Hello?" Teddy had put her on speakerphone and in the background she could hear the sound of his vehicle moving. "Danielle? Is everything okay?"

"I found out who she is!" She pushed herself up from the chair, tossing the blankets onto the floor as she went. She scrolled down the screen, filling him in as she read. "Her name is Alia Harper. She's missing, presumed dead or kidnapped, the investigators aren't sure. Her single mother was found dead in their San Diego apartment from blunt force trauma to the head. Alia was never found."

Teddy whispered a prayer under his breath.

"Alia's parents were never married, and her father's identity is unknown," she added.

"I'm almost home," Teddy said. "I'll be there in a minute. When was she taken?"

"I'm just getting to that. It says December fifteenth…" Her voice trailed off as her mind struggled to process what she was reading. "Nineteen years ago." She stood in the living room, holding her laptop in her hands and staring at the words on the screen. "It's a cold case. She's not a little girl, but a young woman, and she's been missing for almost two decades. But how is this possible? How did a picture from a cold case get inside my bag? I'm going to run the picture through age enhancement software and see if that gets us anywhere. I'll make sure when it's done it emails a copy to both of us."

She loaded up the picture up into the software and started the program running.

The back door clicked. She hadn't realized Teddy had been that close to the house while they'd been talking. She set the laptop down.

"You're home!" she said. "Hey, I'm in the living room!"

"Danielle!" Teddy's voice rose. "That's not me! Get out of the house!"

She turned to run but it was too late. Hal Aberfeldy strode into the living room. He raised a gun in his tattooed hand and pointed it at her face.

"Drop the phone!"

She let it fall and took a step back, feeling the coffee table press up against her legs.

"I warned you not to look for the girl!" He stomped down on her phone and she winced as it cracked. "I told you to let it go. Now, you're coming with me."

No, no she wasn't. Not willingly.

Danielle dived to the side, snatched a lamp off the table and hurled it at him, even as she heard a bullet whiz past her head.

Just let me stay alive until Teddy can get here and save me, Lord.

But a second bullet didn't fly. Instead the man lunged at her, leaping over the table and pounding his fist down into the side of her head so hard she felt it crack against the floor. Pain filled her skull. He grabbed her by the throat stealing the air from her lungs.

"You've been sticking your nose into places it doesn't belong," he said, "and poking around in things that are none of your business. So now you're coming with me. Somebody has some questions for you."

Her hands flailed, reaching for anything she could grab hold of among the debris scattered on the floor—Peg's books, pens and mug—until she felt Peg's emergency alert button. Desperately she tried to flick it into the deep billowing folds of her sleeve, even as she felt herself begin to lose consciousness.

"Danielle!" Teddy burst through the door of his family home with Garfunkel on his heels, calling her name. "Danielle, where are you?"

The signs of a struggle surrounded him. Danielle's laptop and phone looked like someone had stomped on them. He ran from room to room, throwing open doors and searching every corner until he ended right back in the wreck of his living room.

Help me, Lord, where is she? Where do I even look?

His phone buzzed and he grabbed for it, snapping it to his ear and shouting Danielle's name before he realized it wasn't a phone call, but an email. The age enhancement software had sent through a copy of the picture. He opened the file. A wide-eyed young woman with a narrow face and hopeful eyes looked back at him, and thanks to Danielle's brilliant technical work, he knew in an instant who it was—Hailey Bell.

The young woman who worked at Danielle's gym had been the person they'd been looking for all along?

Teddy placed a quick call to his unit and filled Chief Noah Jameson in on the situation, including the fact that he suspected Hailey Bell was cold-case kidnap victim Alia Harper, and the fact that Danielle had been abducted. Noah said he'd send a crime scene unit to Teddy's house and a different team of officers to talk to Hailey. Then he told Teddy to hold tight and pray.

They ended the call and Teddy dropped to his knees and prayed, feeling as if his heart had been turned inside out. He never should've left her alone. Not for fifteen minutes. Not for five. Not even in the safety of his own home. Not while it was possible someone could be after her. A soft whimper made him look down. Garfunkel dropped his head against Teddy's knee. He ran his hand over the dog's neck.

His phone beeped and he glanced in amazement at the screen. One of his mother's two emergency alert trackers was on the move and nowhere near the church where he'd left her. Fear stabbed his heart. He hit his mother's number.

"Hello? Teddy?"

Relief filled his core. "Mom! Are you okay? Where are you?"

"Of course I'm okay," she said. "I'm in the church with Ned."

He blinked. "But where's your emergency alert button?"

"The blue one's here in my purse. I left the green one on the table at home."

He glanced down at the screen and watched as the dot on the map blinked along the highway. It was moving toward the woods.

Fresh hope surged in his pain filled chest. It was Danielle. It had to be.

"Mom, I need you to stay there at the church with Ned and not to go anywhere until I call you later, okay? And pray for Danielle. She's in trouble, but Garfunkel and I are going to find her."

"Will do. You stay safe."

"You too." He ended the call, leaped to his feet and grabbed Garfunkel's leash. "Come on. Let's go find Danielle."

ELEVEN

It was dark and cold in the trunk of the car. Danielle lay on her back, still in her stocking feet and without her gloves or coat. Her fingertips clutched the small emergency alert button she'd managed to swipe and slide into her sleeve, pressing the button down with all her might, praying that Teddy would use it to find her.

She'd fought and struggled against her attacker with every ounce of energy that her body could muster. Until he'd gotten her by the throat and choked her so hard she'd started to feel her head spinning and consciousness slipping away from her. Her body had gone limp and she'd been barely conscious as she'd been dragged out the back door, had her hands tied together and had been tossed in the trunk of the car. Now all she could do was wait, pray and plan.

No one's ever truly lost, she told herself. *Because no matter where they are, they're always in God's sight and held in God's hands.* It was the sentiment that had fueled her work and the hope that would sustain her now. Ever since she'd found the photo of the girl in her bag, she'd prayed that investigators would find her and bring her kidnapper to justice. Danielle now prayed that God would spare her and give her another opportunity to fight for her life, and that she'd know when to seize that opportunity. Then she found herself praying for Teddy. She thanked God for every moment they'd had together—even the ones when they'd been arguing or disagreeing, or she'd felt insecure or weak. He'd been strong for her when she'd needed someone to be. And she liked him. No, more than that, she loved him, even if she hadn't had the courage to admit that to herself before. And no matter what happened next, she prayed this wasn't goodbye.

The car stopped. Cold air whistled outside with the sound of trees shaking their skeletal branches in the wind. She braced herself as she heard the thump of a car door closing and the sound of footsteps crunching on the snowy ground coming toward her. The trunk popped open. Aberfeldy leaned down to grab her. She attacked, screaming at the top of her lungs for help and bicycle kicking up hard with both feet, until she heard the satisfying crack of her heel making contact with his nose. He swore and fell back, just for a moment, clutching his face, and she saw the drip of blood from his fingers, tiny drops falling into the snow at his feet. *DNA.* She'd just made sure he'd left a sample of his DNA.

He yanked a Taser from his pocket, aimed it at her and fired. The two prongs hit her and sent an electric current shooting through her body, paralyzing her. The alert button fell from her hands. She cried out, feeling the electricity rip through her. Then the pain stopped and she lay there a moment, reminding herself that police officers faced Tasers and stun guns firsthand in training to understand what the experience was like. Her colleagues had survived. So would she.

"Let me make one thing clear," Aberfeldy said. "I just need you to talk. I don't need you to be able to walk. I'll drag you through the woods wounded and screaming if I have to. Have I made myself clear?"

Perfectly clear. She nodded. Not trying to find words even if her mouth had wanted to work. He reached in, grabbed her body and hauled her out, half lifting and half throwing her onto the ground. She lay there a moment, feeling the snow sting her bare hands and seep through her socks.

Trees spread out in every direction. Thick snow pelted down, spiraling white against a quickly dimming sky. Night would fall soon and there were no buildings or cars in sight. A sob slipped from her lips. Teddy would find her; she had faith in him just like he'd had faith in her. He'd track the signal on his phone to the car, then Garfunkel would spot the blood drops on the ground and use it to sniff out where the criminal was taking her. She just prayed she'd still be alive until they found her.

Aberfeldy reached into the trunk, yanked open the wheel well and pulled out a shovel. She felt the blood flee her limbs. Wherever he was taking her, he didn't expect her to ever come back.

"Stand up," he said. "Walk."

She stumbled forward as he led her deeper and deeper into the woods. She prayed with every step.

Teddy and Garfunkel would find her. They had to. She had faith.

"Stop here," he said. She looked up to realize they were in a clearing and almost immediately she felt her freezing limbs give way, pitching her forward into the snow. "Someone wants to talk to you."

Here? Who?

Aberfeldy stuck a tablet computer in front of her eyes and she blinked to see an elderly man with a regal bearing sitting up in an armchair, in what looked like a retirement home. Even with his white hair thinning and his once-muscular body frail with age, she recognized him immediately.

It was Ian and Hailey's father, Papa Bell.

Suddenly she felt all the scattered pieces of information and data she'd collected about the missing girl click into place.

Sometimes things weren't as complicated as they seemed.

"Ms. Abbott, my name is Papa Bell…"

"I know who you are," she said, "and I have a pretty good guess that I know what you've done."

Aberfeldy aimed his gun at her over the tablet. "You will answer his questions. Or I'll shoot you."

"You'll shoot me either way." Danielle's eyes darted to him for barely a second then fixed on the screen. "And I have some questions for you, Papa Bell. You murdered Hailey's mother when she was a little girl and then kidnapped Hailey. Didn't you?"

Papa's face went red. "Hailey is my daughter—"

"You kidnapped her!"

"I rescued her!" His voice rose along with his hand as if wanting to strike her through the screen. "She is my child. But her mother tried to keep her from me. I went to her apartment to talk some sense into her. She fell. I took Hailey back to New York with me and gave her a real home with my wife and son!"

And raised her in fear and paranoia, Danielle imagined, together with a wife who she guessed was either on board with the scheme or too frightened of him to confront him, and alongside an older brother, Ian, who also must not have been much more than three or four at the time. Did he remember when his father brought Hailey home to join his family? Had he been too young to remember, or had he blocked out the memories? All this time she'd wondered who'd bullied Ian. Now she wondered if it was his own father.

"Does Ian know?" she asked.

That question seemed to snap Papa back into focus. "No, and he's never going to know. Neither is Hailey."

How was he about to stop them from knowing the truth? Clearly someone suspected already or the picture wouldn't have gotten put into Danielle's bag. Then the thought hit her like a light bulb going on. When Hailey had looked so upset when Danielle had showed her the sketch, had it been because Danielle had just told her the picture had been stolen?

Lord, whatever happens to me, help Hailey and Ian find out the truth.

"You think I don't know Hailey slipped that picture in your bag?" Papa snapped. "I saw her on camera. She found the picture in my late wife's belongings and asked me about it. She wanted to know what beach that was and why she'd never seen any other pictures of herself as a baby. She was clearly suspicious, but she's always been a little paranoid. I told her it was none of her business and that if she knew what was good for her she'd forget all about it."

But if he already knew all that, then why was she here? So he could find out who she'd told? *Teddy and his mother!* Danielle's heart raced in her chest. Papa would've seen Teddy at the gym on the cameras. After he killed her, would he go after them?

"You're going to record a video for me," Papa said. "You're going to apologize to my family for poking your nose in where it doesn't belong and tell my daughter that your research proved that Ian's mother and I are her parents and there's no reason to look into this any further."

Hailey wouldn't believe it. But that wasn't the point, was it? The point was to scare Hailey and keep her trapped and controlled. Just like the security cameras he'd set up around the gym, the constant surveillance, the all-too-convenient fire alarm when Danielle was at the gym. Hailey's frequent upset stomach was suspicious now too. Had her father been poisoning her? Just how far had he gone to keep control of his children? How far was he willing to go to keep Hailey too frightened and dependent to dig any further? If Hailey knew Danielle was lying, it would just make her more afraid. Because after Danielle recorded the message, Papa was going to make her disappear.

"Garfunkel, run!" Teddy pelted though the dense trees, racing after the K-9 dog as he chased the scent through the woods. The tracker had led them to the car. Anguish had pierced Teddy's heart when he'd found it empty. Backup was on its way, but Teddy hadn't waited for them to arrive, because Garfunkel had picked something up—a few tiny drops of blood in the snow—and that had been enough to track. Knowing Danielle, she'd somehow done it on purpose. Now he just had to pray they made it to her on time.

Because I love her, Lord. I should've told her before. Please don't let it be too late.

"Teddy!" He heard her voice rising on the wind toward him, filled with a strength and courage that sent adrenaline pumping though his core. "Teddy! I'm here!"

He didn't know if it was the sound of him and Garfunkel running through the woods or hope that had her shouting out his name.

"I'm coming!" he shouted.

"Watch out! He has a gun!"

No sooner had her words reached his ears than he heard a bullet ripping through the trees toward them, coming within inches of Garfunkel's flank. Teddy yanked his gun from its holster and ordered Garfunkel behind him. A second gunshot cracked. Then the trees parted and Teddy saw them. Danielle was down on her knees in the snow, wet and shivering. Aberfeldy stood over her with gun raised to shoot. He didn't get the opportunity. Teddy fired a single bullet, swift and sure, into the criminal's chest. Aberfeldy crumpled to the ground, dead, his gun and what looked like a computer tablet fell from his hands into the snow. Despite everything he'd done, Teddy prayed God would have mercy on him and all those who'd loved him.

In a heartbeat Teddy reached Danielle, picking her up out of the snow, lifting her and cradling her to his chest as she shuddered and fell against him. For a moment, he just stood there, with his loyal dog by his side and the woman he loved sheltered in his arms.

Thank You, God. Just thank You, God.

"You found me," Danielle said. She tilted her beautiful face up toward his. "You and Garfunkel found me."

"Of course we did." Teddy felt his voice grow husky in his chest. "Remember, I promised that if you ever got lost, I would find you."

A laugh and a sob escaped her lips at once. "And I would find you."

Cradling her tightly to his chest with one arm, he reached into his pocket, pulled out a knife and cut her wrists free. Her hand slid around his neck.

"Now, come on," he said. "Back up is already on its way."

He turned away. But before he could take two steps, the muffled, distant sound of sirens and shouting filtered from below them. He bent down, plucked the computer tablet out of the snow and blinked. A live video was playing. Police were swarming a room and Papa Bell was being arrested. Then Ian's face suddenly filled the screen.

"You found her!" Joy filled Ian's face.

"I did." Teddy held Danielle closer. "How did you even know she was missing?"

"Your police friend told me," Ian said, "when he came to talk to my sister and me, and I wanted to help. The name Hal Aberfeldy rang a bell. My father had used a man with a similar name to collect his debts and intimidate competitors years ago until he'd been arrested for assault, and I wondered if it was the same man. So, I hacked my dad's banking password and found he'd been paying Aberfeldy. Then I led them to my father and they arrested him."

Teddy took a breath. It seemed Danielle had been right to trust Ian.

"Hailey was the girl in the picture," Danielle said. "Your father murdered her mother and stole her when she was little. Also, I think you should check in to whether your father has been poisoning her as a way of keeping her under his thumb."

Ian's face paled and Teddy's heart ached for him.

"I don't know why I'm not more surprised by that," Ian said. "We both used to be sick a lot as children—especially her. I'm now wondering if it was part of our father's attempts to control us. Don't worry, whatever my father did, I'll take care of her and help her through this. I promise."

"I know you will," Danielle said.

Fresh sirens sounded through the woods. Back up had arrived. Teddy ended the call and then took off jogging through the trees, holding Danielle to his chest and with Garfunkel leading the way.

"You're the first man to ever carry me," she said.

"Good." He held her tighter. "I intend to be the last."

He hadn't meant to blurt the words out so quickly, but they were out now and he stood by them. He wanted forever with Danielle. She was one of a kind. She was the most amazing woman he'd ever met and he didn't want to ever imagine himself without her.

Okay, Lord, so I know I love her and want to marry her. How do I convince her to marry me?

But for now Danielle seemed happy to just lay against his chest and closed her eyes as he ran with her through the woods.

The next few hours passed in a blur. Police had come and taken Aberfeldy's body away. Colleagues confirmed that Papa Bell had been arrested. Danielle spoke to both Hailey and Ian on the phone, as brother and sister comforted each other and tried to make sense of what their father had done. And throughout it all, Teddy never left Danielle's side and neither did Garfunkel. She'd become a part of them. She was like a piece of his heart that he hadn't realized was missing until now, but he couldn't imagine ever being without her again.

As night fell, they sat by the Christmas tree back in his living room, with her hand in his and Garfunkel lying on the floor at their feet. Danielle's head fell against his shoulder. His heart was full of questions he didn't have answers to and words he didn't know how to speak.

He loved her but didn't know how to tell her. He wanted a future with her, but didn't know what that would mean for her, himself or his mother. And the fact that Danielle was being uncharacteristically quiet didn't help his nerves much either.

"I'm going out!" His mother's voice filled the room. He looked up. Peg Kowalski was standing in the doorway in her favorite wool coat with a fancy new scarf he'd never seen before around her neck. She waved him down before he could stand. "No, don't get up. Ned is picking me up. We're going out."

Again?

Danielle sat up straight, but she didn't let go of Teddy's hand. "Good night, Mrs. Kowalski."

"Call me Peg, and I hope to see you again soon."

Was this actually happening? Teddy felt like he had water in his ears.

"But Ned can't pick you up," he said. "Ned can't drive."

"I know," she said. "But I told him about that rideshare app Danielle put on my phone and he got his granddaughter to set him up. The car picked him up first and now he's coming to get me."

On their own? Without their children or grandchildren? Hadn't she just seen him yesterday?

"Are you sure you're going to be okay?" he asked.

She laughed. Then she reached into her pocket and pulled out her leather gloves.

"We need to talk sometime, you and me," Peg said. "Because Ned keeps asking me to marry him, and I think I'm going to say yes."

Teddy slid his hand away from Danielle and stood up. Married? His mother was thinking of getting married?

"But you're almost seventy!" Teddy said. "And he must be at least sixty-five!"

"Sixty-eight," his mother said. Her arms crossed. "Are you telling me people my age can't be in love? He's been asking me for years, but I kept telling him, no, my son Teddy needed me too much. He has a great apartment in a very nice building with a dining room, cleaners and medical staff, and everything I need to grow old."

"The same medical staff who just yesterday were trying to keep you from getting dessert?"

"They don't know me yet." Peg shrugged. "And here I thought my son should be thankful somebody else is being overly protective of me for a change."

Well then. Teddy crossed the floor and gave his mother a hug. "If this is what you want, you have my blessing. Not that you need it. Ned seems great and I'm sure you'll be very happy together."

"Me too." His mother's eyes twinkled.

And he stood there, with what he suspected was a goofy and stunned smile on his face, as his mother patted him on the shoulder and, when the car pulled up in the driveway moments later, met Ned at the door and went out into the night.

Teddy turned around slowly and walked back into the living room, feeling like a man in a daze.

"I had no idea my mother was dating Ned. I thought they were just friends." Then he saw the slight smile rise to Danielle's lips. "You knew though! Didn't you? How did you know?"

Danielle sat back against the couch. "I don't know. I suspected. There was just something in the way she talked about him."

He glanced from the dazzling lights of the Christmas tree down to where his K-9 partner lay curled up on the floor at Danielle's feet. Garfunkel looked up as if sensing him. The dog's eyes met his.

Yeah, I'm about to go for it, dude. But this one I gotta do on my own. You understand.

Garfunkel curled back into a ball. The dog's eyes closed. Teddy swallowed hard. Then his gaze rose to the beautiful woman curled up on his couch.

"I've still got a lot to learn about love," Teddy said. He crossed the floor toward her as she rose from the couch to greet him. "I've never dated anyone. Maybe because of how much I thought my mother needed me or because of how very bad her marriage to my father was. But I never brought a woman home, carried anyone in my arms or kissed someone the way I kissed you. I know that love put you through the wringer, Danielle. You went for it, gave it your all, and got chewed up and spit out. But me? I've never even had the guts to try. Or at least, never met anyone who was worth giving my heart to. Before this. Before you."

He reached out his hands toward her. She reached back, her fingertips brushing against his, as slowly her hands slid into his grasp.

"I still have a lot of healing to do," Danielle said. "I don't like how I reacted earlier today about those women at the gym. I'm not beating myself up for it or anything. I just don't want it to always be like that."

"I know." He pulled her closer until she was standing just a breath away from him. "And it won't always be. What is it you told me? Some things take time. It took time for my mother to heal from the emotional scars my father left her with and find a new man to give her heart to. It took time for me to grow and heal from the health problems I was born with."

"It'll take time for Hailey and Ian to heal from what their father did," Danielle interjected.

He felt a smile curl at the corner of his lips. "Yeah, it will. And by the sounds of things they're going to help each other through it. I'm sorry. I don't know if I ever told you that you were right about Ian."

Her smile grew wider. "No worries."

"My point is," he said, "healing takes time. Finding that which is lost takes time. Getting used to my mother leaving home and getting married might take me some time."

"Yeah, it might." She laughed. Then she pulled her hands from his and slid them up around his neck.

"It's going to take you time to learn to trust," he went on. "I want to be standing right here beside you as you do. I want to be the person you talk to when you're worried.

I want to be the person who wraps his arms around you, strokes your hair and tells you it's all going to be okay. I want to be the person you grow with and go on adventures with. I want to be the one you babble on excitedly at about whatever you're working on and the one who brings you food and coffee when you're up working all night. I want to be the man that you deserve, Danielle. If you'll have me."

Her eyes met his and he knew her answer before she opened her mouth.

"And if I ever get lost, you'll come find me?"

He pulled her tighter. "I will. I promise. But you and I will never get lost ever again. I love you, Danielle."

"I love you, Teddy," she whispered. "Merry Christmas."

"Merry Christmas."

And then his lips met hers and kissed any further words or worries from her lips.

* * * * *

Dear Reader,

Thank you so much for joining me for Teddy and Danielle's story! I've really enjoyed getting to know them and it's been such a thrill to contribute a story to the True Blue K-9 Unit continuity and write alongside the other authors in the series. Behind the scenes, series authors work hard at supporting each other in friendship, writing advice and prayer. I love being able to work with them and our incredible editor, Emily Rodmell, to bring stories like these to life.

Both Teddy and Danielle have faced a lot of challenges, but are committed to building the kind of strong relationship together that will last for the rest of their lives.

My prayer for you this Christmas is that you'll be surrounded by people who love and support you whatever you're facing.

Thank you for sharing this journey with me,
Maggie

WE HOPE YOU ENJOYED THIS BOOK!

Love Inspired®
SUSPENSE

Uncover the truth in these thrilling
stories of faith in the face of crime
from Love Inspired Suspense.
Discover six new books available
every month, wherever books
are sold!

LoveInspired.com

Get 4 FREE REWARDS!

We'll send you 2 FREE Books plus 2 FREE Mystery Gifts.

Love Inspired® Suspense books feature Christian characters facing challenges to their faith... and lives.

FREE Value Over **$20**